Ian McEwan was born in Aldershot, Hampshire. He spent much of his childhood in the Far East, Germany and North Africa where his father, an officer in the army, was posted, returning to England to read English at Sussex University. His works have earned him worldwide critical acclaim. He is the recipient of numerous awards, including the 1998 Booker Prize and the 2011 Jerusalem Prize. He was awarded a CBE in 2000. In addition to his prose fiction, McEwan has written plays for television, film screenplays, and opera librettos. Amongst various film adaptations of his novels is *Atonement* (2007), starring James McAvoy and Keira Knightley. McEwan lives in London.

You can discover more about the author at www.ianmcewan.com

THE CHILDREN ACT

Fiona Maye is a leading High Court judge, presiding over cases in the family court. She is renowned for her fierce intelligence, exactitude and sensitivity. But her professional success belies private sorrow and domestic strife. There is the lingering regret of her childlessness, and her marriage of thirty-five years is in crisis. Now she is called on to try an urgent case: for religious reasons, a beautiful seventeen-year-old boy, Adam, is refusing the medical treatment that could save his life, and his devout parents share his wishes. Time is running out. Should the secular court overrule sincerely held faith? In the course of reaching a decision, Fiona visits Adam in hospital — an encounter which stirs long-buried feelings in her and powerful new emotions in the boy. Her judgment has momentous consequences for them both.

IAN McEWAN

◆

THE
CHILDREN
ACT

Complete and Unabridged

CHARNWOOD
Leicester

First published in Great Britain in 2014 by
Jonathan Cape
London

First Charnwood Edition
published 2015
by arrangement with
Jonathan Cape
The Random House Group Limited
London

A catalogue record for this book is available
from the British Library.

ISBN 978–1–4448–2493–3

Published by
F. A. Thorpe (Publishing)
Anstey, Leicestershire

Set by Words & Graphics Ltd.
Anstey, Leicestershire
Printed and bound in Great Britain by
T. J. International Ltd., Padstow, Cornwall

This book is printed on acid-free paper

To Ray Dolan

When a court determines any question with respect to . . . the upbringing of a child . . . the child's welfare shall be the court's paramount consideration.

Section 1(a), the Children Act (1989)

1

London. Trinity term one week old. Implacable June weather. Fiona Maye, a High Court judge, at home on Sunday evening, supine on a chaise longue, staring past her stockinged feet towards the end of the room, towards a partial view of recessed bookshelves by the fireplace and, to one side, by a tall window, a tiny Renoir lithograph of a bather, bought by her thirty years ago for fifty pounds. Probably a fake. Below it, centred on a round walnut table, a blue vase. No memory of how she came by it. Nor when she last put flowers in it. The fireplace not lit in a year. Blackened raindrops falling irregularly into the grate with a ticking sound against balled-up yellowing newsprint. A Bokhara rug spread on wide polished floorboards. Looming at the edge of vision, a baby grand piano bearing silver-framed family photos on its deep black shine. On the floor by the chaise longue, within her reach, the draft of a judgment. And Fiona was on her back, wishing all this stuff at the bottom of the sea.

In her hand was her second Scotch and water. She was feeling shaky, still recovering from a bad moment with her husband. She rarely drank, but the Talisker and tap water was a balm, and she thought she might cross the room to the sideboard for a third. Less Scotch, more water, for she was in court tomorrow and she was duty judge now, available for any sudden demand, even as she lay recuperating. He had made a shocking declaration and placed an impossible burden on her. For the first time in years, she had actually shouted, and some faint echo still resounded in her ears. 'You idiot! You fucking *idiot*!' She had not sworn out loud since her carefree teenage visits to Newcastle, though a potent word sometimes intruded on her thoughts when she heard self-serving evidence or an irrelevant point of law.

And then, not long after that, wheezy with outrage, she had said loudly, at least twice, 'How *dare* you!'

It was hardly a question, but he answered it calmly. 'I need it. I'm fifty-nine. This is my last shot. I've yet to hear evidence for an afterlife.'

A pretentious remark and she had been lost for a reply. She simply stared at him, and perhaps her mouth was open. In the spirit of the staircase, she had a response now, on the chaise longue. 'Fifty-nine? Jack, you're *sixty*! It's pathetic, it's banal.'

What she had actually said, lamely, was, 'This is too ridiculous.'

'Fiona, when did we last make love?'

When did they? He had asked this before, in moods plaintive to querulous. But the crowded recent past can be difficult to recall. The Family Division teemed with strange differences, special pleading, intimate half-truths, exotic accusation. And as in all branches of law, fine-grained particularities of circumstance needed to be assimilated at speed. Last week, she heard final

2

submissions from divorcing Jewish parents, unequally Orthodox, disputing their daughters' education. The draft of her completed judgment was on the floor beside her. Tomorrow, coming before her again would be a despairing Englishwoman, gaunt, pale, highly educated, mother of a five-year-old girl, convinced, despite assurances to the court to the contrary, that her daughter was about to be removed from the jurisdiction by the father, a Moroccan business-man and strict Muslim, to a new life in Rabat, where he intended to settle. Otherwise, routine wrangles over residence of children, over houses, pensions, earnings, inheritance. It was the larger estates that came to the High Court. Wealth mostly failed to bring extended happiness. Parents soon learned the new vocabulary and patient procedures of the law, and were dazed to find themselves in vicious combat with the one they once loved. And waiting offstage, boys and girls first-named in the court documents, troubled little Bens and Sarahs, huddling together while the gods above them fought to the last, from the Family Proceedings Court, to the High Court, to the Court of Appeal.

All this sorrow had common themes, there was a human sameness to it, but it continued to fascinate her. She believed she brought reason-ableness to hopeless situations. On the whole, she believed in the provisions of family law. In her optimistic moments she took it as a significant marker in civilisation's progress, to fix in the statutes the child's needs above its parents'. Her days were full, and in the evenings

3

recently, various dinners, something at Middle Temple for a retiring colleague, a concert at Kings Place (Schubert, Scriabin), and taxis, Tube trains, dry-cleaning to collect, a letter to draft about a special school for the cleaning lady's autistic son, and finally sleep. Where was the sex? At that moment, she couldn't recall.

'I don't keep a record.'

He spread his hands, resting his case.

She had watched as he crossed the room and poured himself a measure of Scotch, the Talisker she was drinking now. Lately, he was looking taller, easier in his movements. While his back was turned to her she had a cold premonition of rejection, of the humiliation of being left for a young woman, of being left behind, useless and alone. She wondered if she should simply go along with anything he wanted, then rejected the thought.

He had come back towards her with his glass. He wasn't offering her a Sancerre the way he usually did around this time.

'What do you want, Jack?'

'I'm going to have this affair.'

'You want a divorce.'

'No. I want everything the same. No deception.'

'I don't understand.'

'Yes you do. Didn't you once tell me that couples in long marriages aspire to the condition of siblings? We've arrived, Fiona. I've become your brother. It's cosy and sweet and I love you, but before I drop dead, I want one big passionate affair.'

Mistaking her amazed gasp for laughter, for mockery perhaps, he said roughly, 'Ecstasy, almost blacking out with the thrill of it. Remember that? I want one last go, even if you don't. Or perhaps you do.'

She stared at him in disbelief.

'There it is then.'

This was when she had found her voice and told him what kind of idiot he was. She had a powerful grip on what was conventionally correct. That he had, as far as she knew, always been faithful, made his proposition all the more outrageous. Or if he'd deceived her in the past he'd done it brilliantly. She already knew the name of the woman. Melanie. Not so remote from the name of a fatal form of skin cancer. She knew she could be obliterated by his affair with this twenty-eight-year-old statistician.

'If you do this it'll be the end for us. It's as simple as that.'

'Is this a threat?'

'My solemn promise.'

By then she had regained her temper. And it did seem simple. The moment to propose an open marriage was before the wedding, not thirty-five years later. To risk all they had so that he might relive a passing sensual thrill! When she tried to imagine wanting something like it for herself — her 'last fling' would be her first — she could think only of disruption, assignations, disappointment, ill-timed phone calls. The sticky business of learning to be with someone new in bed, newly devised endearments, all the fakery. Finally, the necessary disentangling, the effort required to be open and sincere. And nothing quite the same when she came away. No, she preferred an imperfect existence, the one she had now.

But on the chaise longue it rose before her, the true extent of the insult, how he was prepared to pay for his pleasures with her misery. Ruthless. She had seen him single-minded at the expense of others, most often in a good cause. This was new. What had changed? He had stood erect, feet well apart as he poured his single malt, the fingers of his free hand moving to a tune in his head, some shared song perhaps, not shared with her. Hurting her and not caring — that was new. He had always been kind, loyal and kind, and kindness, the Family Division daily proved, was the essential human ingredient. She had the power to remove a child from an unkind parent and she sometimes did. But remove herself from an unkind husband? When she was weak and desolate? Where was her protective judge?

Self-pity in others embarrassed her, and she wouldn't have it now. She was having a third drink instead. But she poured only a token measure, added much water and returned to her couch. Yes, it had been the kind of conversation of which she should have taken notes. Important to remember, to measure the insult carefully. When she threatened to end the marriage if he went ahead, he had simply repeated himself, told her again how he loved her, always would, that there was no other life but this, that his unmet sexual needs caused him great unhappiness, that there was this one chance and he wanted to take it with her knowledge and, so he hoped, her assent. He was speaking to her in the spirit of openness. He could have done it 'behind her back'. Her thin, unforgiving back.

'Oh,' she murmured. 'That's decent of you, Jack.'

'Well, actually . . . ' he said, and didn't finish.

She guessed he was about to tell her the affair had already begun and she couldn't bear to hear it. Didn't need to. She saw it. A pretty statistician working on the diminishing probability of a man returning to an embittered wife. She saw a sunlit morning, an unfamiliar bathroom, and Jack, still decently muscled, pulling a half-unbuttoned clean white linen shirt over his head in that impatient way he had, a discarded shirt tossed towards the laundry basket hanging by one arm before sliding to the floor. Perdition. It would happen, with or without her consent.

'The answer's no.' She had used a rising tone, like a flinty schoolmarm. She added, 'What else would you expect me to say?'

She felt helpless and wanted the conversation to end. There was a judgment to approve before tomorrow for publication in the *Family Law Reports*. The fates of two Jewish schoolgirls had already been settled in the ruling she had delivered in court, but the prose needed to be smoothed, as did the respect owed to piety in order to be proof against an appeal. Outside, summer rain beat against the windows; distantly, from beyond Gray's Inn Square, tyres hissed on drenched asphalt. He would leave her and the world would go on.

His face had been tight as he shrugged and turned to leave the room. At the sight of his retreating back, she felt the same cold fear. She would have called after him but for the dread of being ignored. And what could she say? Hold me, kiss me, have the girl. She had listened to his footsteps down the hall, their bedroom door closing firmly, then silence settling over their flat, silence and the rain that hadn't stopped in a month.

★ ★ ★

First the facts. Both parties were from the tight folds of the strictly observant Chareidi community in north London. The Bernsteins' marriage was arranged by their parents, with no expectation of dissent. Arranged, not forced, both parties, in rare accord, insisted. Thirteen years on, all agreed, mediator, social worker and judge included, that here was a marriage beyond repair. The couple were now separated. Between them they managed with difficulty the care of the two children, Rachel and Nora, who lived with the mother and had extensive contact with the father. Marriage breakdown had started in the early years. After the difficult birth of the second girl, the mother was unable to conceive again, due to radical surgery. The father had set his heart on a large family and thus began the painful unravelling. After a period of depression (prolonged, said the father; brief, said the mother), she studied at the Open University, gained a good qualification and entered on a career in teaching at primary level once the younger had started school. This arrangement did not suit the father or the many relatives. Within the Chareidim, whose traditions were unbroken for centuries, women were expected to raise children, the more the better, and look after the home. A university degree and a job were highly unusual. A senior figure of good standing in the community was called as a witness by the father and said as much.

Men did not receive much education either. From their mid teens, they were expected to give most of their time to studying the Torah. Generally, they did not go to university. Partly for this reason, many Chareidim were of modest means. But not the Bernsteins, though they would be when their lawyers' bills were settled. A grandparent with a share in a patent for an olive-pitting machine had settled money on the couple jointly. They expected to spend everything they had on their respective silks, both women well known to the judge. On the surface, the dispute concerned Rachel and Nora's schooling. However, at stake was the entire context of the girls' growing up. It was a fight for their souls.

Chareidi boys and girls were educated separately to preserve their purity. Modish clothes, television and the internet were forbidden, and so was mixing with children who were allowed such distractions. Homes that did not observe strict kosher rules were out of bounds. Every aspect of daily existence was well covered by established customs. The problem had started with the mother, who was breaking with the community, though not with Judaism. Against the father's objections, she was already sending the girls to a co-educational Jewish secondary school where television, pop music, the internet and mixing with non-Jewish children were permitted. She wanted her girls to stay on at school past the age of sixteen and to go to university if they wished. In her written evidence she said she wanted her daughters to know more about how others lived, to be socially tolerant, to have the career opportunities she never had, and as adults to be economically self-sufficient, with the chance of meeting the sort of husband with professional skills who could help to support a family. Unlike her husband, who gave all his time to studying, and teaching the Torah eight hours a week without pay.

For all the reasonableness of her case, Judith Bernstein — angular pale face, uncovered frizzy ginger hair fastened with a huge blue clasp — was not an easy presence in court. A constant passing forwards with freckly agitated fingers of notes to her counsel, much muted sighing, eye-rolling and lip-pursing whenever her husband's counsel spoke, inappropriate rummaging and jiggling in an outsized camel leather handbag, removing from it at one low point in a long afternoon a pack of cigarettes and a lighter — provocative items in her husband's scheme, surely — and lining them up side by side, on hand for when the court rose. Fiona saw all this from her advantage of height but pretended not to.

Mr Bernstein's written evidence was intended to persuade the judge that his wife was a selfish woman with 'anger-management problems' (in the Family Division, a common, often mutual charge) who had turned her back on her marriage vows, argued with his parents and her community, cutting the girls off from both. On the contrary, Judith said from the stand, it was her parents-in-law who would not see her or the children until they had returned to the proper way of life, disowned the modern world, including social media, and until she kept a home that was kosher by their terms.

Mr Julian Bernstein, reedily tall, like one of the rushes that hid the infant Moses, apologetically stooped over court papers, sidelocks stirring moodily as his barrister accused his wife of being unable to separate her own needs from the children's. What she said they needed was whatever she wanted for herself. She was wrenching the girls away from a warmly secure and familiar environment, disciplined but loving, whose rules and observances provided for every contingency, whose identity was clear, its methods proven through the generations, and whose members were generally happier and more fulfilled than those of the secular consumerist world outside — a world that mocked the spiritual life and whose mass culture denigrated girls and women. Her ambitions were frivolous, her methods disrespectful, even destructive. She loved her children far less than she loved herself.

To which Judith responded huskily that nothing denigrated a person, boy or girl, more than the denial of a decent education and the dignity of proper work; that all through her childhood and teenage years she had been told that her only purpose in life was to run a nice home for her husband and care for his children — and that too was a denigration of her right to choose a purpose for herself. When she pursued, with great difficulty, her studies at the Open University, she faced ridicule, contempt and anathemas. She had promised herself that the girls would not suffer the same limitations.

The opposing barristers were in tactical agreement (because it was plainly the judge's view) that the issue was not merely a matter of education. The court must choose, on behalf of the children, between total religion and something a little less. Between cultures, identities, states of mind, aspirations, sets of family relations, fundamental definitions, basic loyalties, unknowable futures.

In such matters there lurked an innate predisposition in favour of the status quo, as long as it appeared benign. The draft of Fiona's judgment was twenty-one pages long, spread in a wide fan face down on the floor, waiting for her to take it up, a sheet at a time, to mark with soft pencil.

No sound from the bedroom, nothing but the susurrus of traffic gliding through the rain. She resented the way she was listening out for him, her attention poised, holding its breath, for the creak of the door or a floorboard. Wanting it, dreading it.

Among fellow judges, Fiona Maye was

praised, even in her absence, for crisp prose, almost ironic, almost warm, and for the compact terms in which she laid out a dispute. The Lord Chief Justice himself was heard to observe of her in a murmured aside at lunch, 'Godly distance, devilish understanding, and still beautiful.' Her own view was that with each passing year she inclined a little more to an exactitude some might have called pedantry, to the unassailable definition that might pass one day into frequent citation, like Hoffmann in *Piglowska* v. *Piglowski*, or Bingham or Ward or the indispensable Scarman, all of whom she had made use of here. Here being the limp, unperused first page hanging from her fingers. Was her life about to change? Were learned friends soon to be murmuring in awe over lunch here, or in Lincoln's or Inner or Middle Temple, *And then she threw him out?* Out of the delightful Gray's Inn flat, where she would sit alone until at last the rent, or the years, mounting like the sullen tidal Thames, swept her out too?

Back to her business. Section one: 'Background'. After routine observations about the family's living arrangements, about residence of the children and contact with the father, she described in a separate paragraph the Chareidi community, and how within it religious practice was a total way of life. The distinction between what was rendered to Caesar and what to God was meaningless, much as it was for observant Muslims. Her pencil hovered. To cast Muslim and Jew as one, might that seem unnecessary or provocative, at least to the father? Only if he was

13

unreasonable, and she thought he was not. Stet.

Her second section was entitled 'Moral differences'. The court was being asked to choose an education for two young girls, to choose between values. And in cases like this one, an appeal to what was generally acceptable in society at large was of little help. It was here she invoked Lord Hoffmann. 'These are value judgements on which reasonable people may differ. Since judges are also people, this means that some degree of diversity in their application of values is inevitable . . . '

Over the page, in her lately developing taste for the patient, exacting digression, Fiona devoted several hundred words to a definition of welfare, and then a consideration of the standards to which such welfare might be held. She followed Lord Hailsham in allowing the term to be inseparable from well-being and to include all that was relevant to a child's development as a person. She acknowledged Tom Bingham in accepting that she was obliged to take a medium- and long-term view, noting that a child today might well live into the twenty-second century. She quoted from an 1893 judgment by Lord Justice Lindley to the effect that welfare was not to be gauged in purely financial terms, or merely by reference to physical comfort. She would take the widest possible view. Welfare, happiness, well-being must embrace the philosophical concept of the good life. She listed some relevant ingredients, goals towards which a child might grow. Economic and moral freedom, virtue, compassion and altruism, satisfying work through engagement with demanding tasks, a flourishing network of personal relationships, earning the esteem of others, pursuing larger meanings to one's existence, and having at the centre of one's life one or a small number of significant relations defined above all by love.

Yes, by this last essential she herself was failing. The Scotch and water in a tumbler at her side was untouched, the sight of its urinous yellow, its intrusive corky smell, now repelled her. She should be angrier, she should be talking to an old friend — she had several — she should be striding into the bedroom, demanding to know more. But she felt shrunken to a geometrical point of anxious purpose. Her judgment must be ready for printing by tomorrow's deadline, she must work. Her personal life was nothing. Or should have been. Her attention remained divided between the page in her hand and, fifty feet away, the closed bedroom door. She made herself read a long paragraph, one she had been dubious about at the moment she had spoken it aloud in court. But no harm in a robust statement of the obvious. Well-being was *social*. The intricate web of a child's relationships with family and friends was the crucial ingredient. No child an island. Man a social animal, in Aristotle's famous construction. With four hundred words on this theme, she put to sea, with learned references (Adam Smith, John Stuart Mill) filling her sails. The kind of civilised reach every good judgment needs.

And next, well-being was a *mutable* concept, to be evaluated by the standards of the

15

reasonable man or woman of today. What sufficed a generation ago might now fall short. And again, it was no business of the secular court to decide between religious beliefs or theological differences. All religions were deserving of respect provided they were, in Lord Justice Purchas's phrase, 'legally and socially acceptable' and not, in Lord Justice Scarman's darker formulation, 'immoral or socially obnoxious'.

Courts should be slow to intervene in the interests of the child against the religious principles of the parents. Sometimes they must. But when? In reply, she invoked one of her favourites, wise Lord Justice Munby in the Court of Appeal. 'The infinite variety of the human condition preclude sarbitrary definition.' The admirable Shakespearean touch. *Nor custom stale her infinite variety.* The words derailed her. She knew the speech of Enobarbus by heart, having played him once as a law student, an all-female affair on a lawn in Lincoln's Inn Fields one sunny midsummer's afternoon. When the burden of Bar exams had recently been lifted from her aching back. Around that time, Jack fell in love with her, and not long after, she with him. Their first lovemaking was in a borrowed attic room that roasted under its roof in the afternoon sun. An unopenable porthole window gave a view east of a slice of Thames towards the Pool of London.

She thought of his proposed or actual lover, his statistician, Melanie — she had met her once — a silent young woman with heavy amber beads and a taste for the kind of stilettos that

16

could wreck an old oak floor. *Other women cloy/The appetites they feed, but she makes hungry/Where most she satisfies.* It could be just like that, a poisonous obsession, an addiction drawing him away from home, bending him out of shape, consuming all they had of past and future, as well as present. Or Melanie belonged, as Fiona herself clearly did, with 'other women', the ones who cloy, and he would be back within the fortnight, appetite sated, making plans for the family holiday.

Either way, unbearable.

Unbearable and fascinating. And irrelevant. She forced herself back to her pages, to her summary of the evidence from both parties — efficient and drily sympathetic enough. Next, her account of the court-appointed social worker's report. A plump, well-intentioned young woman often out of breath, uncombed hair, untucked unbuttoned blouse. Chaotic, twice late for the proceedings, due to some complicated trouble with car keys and documents locked in her car and a child to collect from school. But in place of the usual please-both-parties dither, the Cafcass woman's account was sensible, even incisive, and Fiona quoted her with approval. Next?

She looked up and saw her husband on the other side of the room, pouring another drink, a big one, three fingers, perhaps four. And barefoot now, as he, the bohemian academic, often was indoors in summer. Hence the quiet entrance. Likely he had been lying on the bed, regarding for half an hour the lacy ceiling mouldings,

17

reflecting on her unreasonableness. The hunched tension of the shoulders, the way he returned the stopper — a smack with the heel of his thumb — suggested that he had padded in for an argument. She knew the signs.

He turned and came towards her with his undiluted drink. The Jewish girls, Rachel and Nora, must hover behind her like Christian angels and wait. Their secular god had troubles of her own. From her low perspective, she had a decent view of his toenails — nicely trimmed and squared off, bright and youthful half-moons, no sign of the fungal streaks that stained her own toes. He kept in shape with faculty tennis and a set of weights in his study, which he aimed to raise a hundred times in the course of every day. She did little more than haul her bag of documents through the Courts of Justice to her room, taking the stairs rather than the lift. He was handsome in an unruly way, lopsidedly square-jawed, a toothy game-for-anything expression that charmed his students, who didn't expect a dissolute look in a professor of ancient history. She had never thought he laid a finger on the kids. Now, everything looked different. Perhaps, for all a lifetime's entanglement in human weakness, she remained an innocent, mindlessly exempting herself and Jack from the general condition. His only book for the non-academic reader, a pacy life of Julius Caesar, made him briefly almost famous in a muted, respectable fashion. Some pert little second-year minx might have irresistibly put herself in his way. There was, or there used to be, a couch in his office. And a Ne Pas

18

Déranger sign taken from the Hôtel de Crillon at the end of their long-ago honeymoon. These were new thoughts, this was how the worm of suspicion infested the past.

He sat down in the nearest chair. 'You couldn't answer my question so I'll tell you. It's been seven weeks and a day. Are you honestly content with that?'

She said quietly, 'Are you already having this affair?'

He knew that a difficult question was best answered by another. 'You think we're too old? Is that it?'

She said, 'Because if you are I'd like you to pack a bag now and leave.'

A self-harming move, without premeditation, her rook for his knight, utter folly, and no way back. If he stayed, humiliation, if he left, the abyss.

He was settling into his chair, a studded, wood and leather piece with a look of medieval torture about it. She had never liked Victorian Gothic, and never less than now. He crossed his ankle over his knee, his head was cocked as he looked at her in tolerance or pity, and she looked away. Seven weeks and a day also had a medieval ring, like a sentence handed down from an old Court of Assize. It troubled her to think that she might have a case to answer. They'd had a decent sex life for many years, regular and lustily uncomplicated, on weekdays in the early morning just as they woke, before the dazzling concerns of the working day penetrated the heavy bedroom curtains. At weekends in the afternoons, sometimes after tennis, social doubles in Mecklenburgh Square. Obliterating all blame for one's partner's fluffed shots. In fact, a deeply pleasurable love life, and functional, in that it delivered them smoothly into the rest of their existence, and beyond discussion, which was one of its joys. Not even a vocabulary for it — one reason why it pained her to hear him mention it now and why she barely noted the slow decline of ardour and frequency.

But she had always loved him, was always affectionate, loyal, attentive, only last year had nursed him tenderly when he broke his leg and wrist in Méribel during a ridiculous downhill ski race against old school friends. She pleasured him, sat astride him, now she remembered, while he lay grinning amid the chalky splendour of his plaster of Paris. She did not know how to refer to such things in her own defence, and besides, these were not the grounds on which she was being attacked. It was not devotion she lacked but passion.

Then there was age. Not the full withering, not just yet, but its early promise was shining through, just as one might catch in a certain light a glimpse of the adult in a ten-year-old's face. If Jack, sprawled across from her, seemed absurd in this conversation, then how much more so must she appear to him. His white chest hair, of which he remained proud, curled out over his shirt's top button only to declare that it was no longer black; the head hair, thinning monkishly in the familiar pattern, he had grown long in unconvincing compensation; shanks less muscular, not quite filling out his jeans, the eyes holding a gentle hint of future vacancy, with a matching hollowness about the cheeks. So what then of her ankles thickening in coquettish reply, her backside swelling like summer cumulus, her waist waxing stout as her gums receded? All this still in paranoid millimetres. Far worse, the special insult the years reserved for certain women, as the corners of her mouth began their downward turn in pursuit of a look of constant reproach. Fair enough in a bewigged judge frowning at counsel from her throne. But in a lover?

And here they were, like teenagers, shaping up to discuss themselves in the cause of Eros.

Tactically astute, he ignored her ultimatum. Instead he said, 'I don't think we should give up, do you?'

'You're the one who's walking away.'

'I think you have a part in this too.'

'I'm not the one about to wreck our marriage.'

'So you say.'

He said it reasonably, projecting the three words deep into the cave of her self-doubt, shaping them to her inclination to believe that in any conflict as embarrassing as this, she was likely to be wrong.

He took a careful sip of his drink. He was not going to get drunk in order to assert his needs. He would be grave and rational when she would have preferred him loudly in the wrong.

Holding her gaze he said, 'You know I love you.'

'But you'd like someone younger.'

'I'd like a sex life.'

Her cue to make warm promises, draw him back to her, apologise for being busy or tired or unavailable. But she looked away and said nothing. She was not going to dedicate herself under pressure to revive a sensual life she had at that moment no taste for. Especially when she suspected the affair had already begun. He had not troubled himself to deny it, and she was not going to ask again. It was not only pride. She still dreaded his reply.

'Well,' he said after their long pause. 'Wouldn't you?'

'Not with this gun to my head.'

'Meaning?'

'I shape up or you go to Melanie.'

She assumed he had understood her meaning well enough but had wanted to hear her say the woman's name, which she had never spoken out loud before. It evinced a tremor or a tightening in his face, a helpless little tic of arousal. Or it was the naked phrasing, the 'go to'. Had she lost him already? She felt suddenly dizzy, as though her blood pressure had dipped then soared. She pushed herself upright on the chaise longue, and set down on the carpet the page of the judgment still in her hand.

'That's not how it is,' he was saying. 'Look, turn this around. Suppose you were in my place and I was in yours. What would you do?'

'I wouldn't go and find myself a man and then open negotiations with you.'

'What then?'

'I'd find out what was troubling you.' Her voice sounded prim in her ears.

22

He gestured towards her ⌐
'Fine!' The Socratic met⌐
on his students. 'So what i⌐
    For all the stupidity an⌐
exchange, it was the only ⌐
invited it, but she felt i⌐
condescended to, and for the m⌐
reply and instead looked past ⌐
room to the piano, barely played ⌐
and the silver-framed photos it s⌐
country-house style. Both sets of p⌐
wedding day to dotage, his three sistei⌐
brothers, their wives and husbands pre⌐
past (disloyally, they struck no one off),⌐
nephews and nieces, then the thirteen ch⌐
they in turn had made. Life acceleratin⌐
people a small village clustered on a baby gra⌐
She and Jack had contributed nothing, no on⌐
beyond family reunions, near-weekly birthda⌐
presents, multi-generational holidays in the
cheaper sort of castle. In their apartment, they
hosted much family. At the end of the hallway
was a walk-in cupboard filled with folded-up cot,
high chair and playpen, and three wicker baskets
of chewed and fading toys in readiness for the
next addition. And this summer's castle, ten
miles north of Ullapool, awaited their decision.
According to the ill-printed brochure, a moat, a
working drawbridge and a dungeon with hooks
and iron rings in the wall. Yesterday's torture was
now a thrill for the under-twelves. She thought
again of the medieval sentence, seven weeks and
a day, a period that began with the final stages of
the Siamese twins case.

e horror and pity, and the dilemma itself,
the photograph, shown to the judge and
else. Infant sons of Jamaican and Scottish
s lay top-and-tailed amid a tangle of
pport systems on a paediatric intensive-
ed, joined at the pelvis and sharing a single
, their splayed legs at right angles to their
es, in resemblance of a many-pointed star-
. A measure fixed along the side of the incubator
wed this helpless, all too human ensemble to
sixty centimetres in length. Their spinal cords
d the base of their spines were fused, their eyes
losed, four arms raised in surrender to the court's
decision. Their apostolic names, Matthew and
Mark, had not encouraged clear thinking in some
quarters. Matthew's head was swollen, his ears
mere indentations in roseate skin. Mark's head,
beneath the neonatal woollen cap, was normal.
They shared only one organ, their bladder, which
was mostly in Mark's abdomen and which, a
consultant noted, 'emptied spontaneously and
freely through two separate urethras'. Matthew's
heart was large but 'it barely squeezed'. Mark's
aorta fed into Matthew's and it was Mark's heart
that sustained them both. Matthew's brain was
severely malformed and not compatible with normal
development, his chest cavity lacked functional
lung tissue. He had, one of the nursing staff said,
'not the lungs to cry with'.

Mark was sucking normally, feeding and breathing for both, doing 'all the work' and therefore
abnormally thin. Matthew, with nothing to do,
was gaining weight. Left alone, Mark's heart
would sooner or later fail from the effort, and

both must die. Matthew was unlikely to live more than six months. When he died, he would take his brother with him. A London hospital was urgently looking for permission to separate the twins to save Mark, who had the potential to be a normal healthy child. To do so, surgeons would have to clamp then sever the shared aorta, so killing Matthew. And then begin a complicated set of reconstructive procedures on Mark. The loving parents, devout Catholics living in a village on Jamaica's north coast, calm in their belief, refused to sanction murder. God gave life and only God could take it away.

In part, her memory was of a prolonged and awful din assaulting her concentration, a thousand car alarms, a thousand witches in a frenzy, giving substance to the cliché: the screaming headline. Doctors, priests, television and radio hosts, newspaper columnists, colleagues, relations, taxi drivers, the nation at large had a view. The narrative ingredients were compelling: tragic babies, kind-hearted, solemn and eloquent parents in love with each other as well as their children, life, love, death and a race against time. Masked surgeons pitched against supernatural belief. As for the spectrum of positions, at one end were those of secular utilitarian persuasion, impatient of legal detail, blessed by an easy moral equation: one child saved better than two dead. At the other, stood those of firm knowledge not only of God's existence but an understanding of his will. Quoting Lord Justice Ward, Fiona reminded all parties in the opening lines of her judgment, 'This court is a court of law, not of morals, and

25

our task has been to find, and our duty is then to apply, the relevant principles of law to the situation before us — a situation which is unique.'

In this dire contest there was only one desirable or less undesirable outcome, but a lawful route to it was not easy. Under pressure of time, with a noisy world waiting, she found, in just under a week and thirteen thousand words, a plausible way. Or at least, the Court of Appeal, working to an even harsher deadline on the day after she delivered her judgment, seemed to suggest she had. However, there could be no presumption that one life was worth more than another. Separating the twins would be to kill Matthew. Not separating them would, by omission, kill both. The legal and moral space was tight and the matter had to be set as a choice of the lesser evil. Still, the judge was obliged to consider what was in Matthew's best interests. Clearly not death. But nor was life an option. He had a rudimentary brain, no lungs, a useless heart, was probably in pain and condemned to die, and soon.

Fiona argued, in a novel formulation which the Court of Appeal accepted, that Matthew, unlike his brother, had no interests.

But if the lesser evil was preferable, it might still be unlawful. How was murder, cutting open Matthew's body to sever an aorta, to be justified? Fiona rejected the notion urged on her by the hospital's counsel, that separating the twins was analogous to turning off Matthew's life-support machine, which was Mark. The surgery was too invasive, too much of a trespass on Matthew's bodily integrity, to be considered a withdrawal of treatment. Instead, she found her argument in the 'doctrine of necessity', an idea established in common law that in certain limited circumstances, which no parliament would ever care to define, it was permissible to break the criminal law to prevent a greater evil. She referred to a case in which men hijacked a plane to London, terrorised the passengers and were found innocent of any crime because they were acting to avoid persecution in their own country.

Regarding the all-important matter of intent, the purpose of the surgery was not to kill Matthew but to save Mark. Matthew, in all his helplessness, was killing Mark and the doctors must be allowed to come to Mark's defence to remove a threat of fatal harm. Matthew would perish after the separation not because he was purposefully murdered, but because on his own he was incapable of flourishing.

The Court of Appeal agreed, the parents' appeal was dismissed and two days later, at seven in the morning, the twins entered the operating theatre.

The colleagues Fiona valued most sought her out to shake her hand, or wrote the kind of letters worth saving in a special folder. Her judgment was elegant and correct, was the insiders' view. Reconstructive surgery on Mark was successful, public interest faded and moved on. But she was unhappy, couldn't leave the case alone, was awake at nights for long hours, turning over the details, rephrasing certain passages of her judgment, taking another tack. Or she lingered over familiar themes, including her own childlessness. At the same time, there began to arrive in small pastel-coloured envelopes the venomous thoughts of the devout. They were of the view that both children should have been left to die and were not pleased by her decision. Some deployed abusive language, some said they longed to do her physical harm. A few of those claimed to know where she lived.

Those intense weeks left their mark on her, and it had only just faded. What exactly had troubled her? Her husband's question was her own, and he was waiting for an answer now. Before the hearing she had received a submission from the Roman Catholic Archbishop of Westminster. In her judgment she noted in a respectful paragraph that the archbishop preferred Mark to die along with Matthew in order not to interfere with God's purpose. That churchmen should want to obliterate the potential of a meaningful life in order to hold a theological line did not surprise or concern her. The law itself had similar problems when it allowed doctors to suffocate, dehydrate or starve certain hopeless patients to death, but would not permit the instant relief of a fatal injection.

At nights her thoughts returned to that photograph of the twins and the dozen others she had studied, and to the detailed technical information she had heard from medical specialists on all that was wrong with the babies, on the cutting and breaking, splicing and folding of infant flesh they must perform to give Mark a normal life, reconstructing internal organs, rotating his legs, his genitals and bowels through ninety degrees. In the bedroom darkness, while Jack at her side quietly snored, she seemed to peer over a cliff edge. She saw in the remembered pictures of Matthew and Mark a blind and purposeless nullity. A microscopic egg had failed to divide in time due to a failure somewhere along a chain of chemical events, a tiny disturbance in a cascade of protein reactions. A molecular event ballooned like an exploding universe, out onto the wider scale of human misery. No cruelty, nothing avenged, no ghost moving in mysterious ways. Merely a gene transcribed in error, an enzyme recipe skewed, a chemical bond severed. A process of natural wastage as indifferent as it was pointless. Which only brought into relief healthy, perfectly formed life, equally contingent, equally without purpose. Blind luck, to arrive in the world with your properly formed parts in the right place, to be born to parents who were loving, not cruel, or to escape, by geographical or social accident, war or poverty. And therefore to find it so much easier to be virtuous.

For a while, the case had left her numb, caring less, feeling less, going about her business, telling no one. But she became squeamish about bodies, barely able to look at her own or Jack's without feeling repelled. How was she to talk about this? Hardly plausible, to have told him that at this stage of a legal career, this one case among so many others, its sadness, its visceral details and loud public interest, could affect her so intimately. For a while, some part of her had gone cold, along with poor Matthew. She was the one who had dispatched a child from the world, argued him out of existence in thirty-four elegant pages. Never mind that with his bloated head and unsqueezing heart he was doomed to die. She was no less irrational than the archbishop, and had come to regard the shrinking within herself as her due. The feeling had passed, but it left scar tissue in the memory, even after seven weeks and a day.

Not having a body, floating free of physical constraint, would have suited her best.

★ ★ ★

The click of Jack's tumbler against a glass table returned her to the room and his question. He was looking at her steadily. Even if she'd known how to frame a confession, she was in no mood for one. Or any display of weakness. She had work to do, the conclusion to her judgment to proofread, with the angels waiting. Her state of mind was not the issue. The problem was the choice her husband was making, the pressure he was now applying. She was suddenly angry again.

'For the last time, Jack. Are you seeing her? I'll take your silence as a yes.'

But he too was roused, out of his chair, walking away from her to the piano, where he paused, one hand resting on the raised lid, gathering his patience before he turned. In that moment the silence between them expanded. The rain had ceased, the oak trees in the Walks were stilled.

'I thought I'd made myself clear. I'm trying to be open with you. I saw her for lunch. Nothing's happened. I wanted to talk to you first, I wanted — '

'Well you have, and you've had your answer. So what now?'

'Now you tell me what's happened to you.'

'When was this lunch? Where?'

'Last week, at work. It was nothing.'

'The sort of nothing that leads to an affair.'

He remained at the far end of the room. 'There it is,' he said. His tone was flat. A reasonable man tested to exhaustion. Amazing, the theatrics he thought he could get away with. In her time on circuit, ageing and illiterate recidivists, some with very few teeth, had come before her and performed better, thinking aloud from the dock.

'There it is,' he repeated. 'And I'm sorry.'

'Do you realise what you're about to destroy?'

'I could say the same. Something's going on and you won't talk to me.'

Let him go, a voice, her own voice, said in her thoughts. And immediately, the same old fear gripped her. She couldn't, she did not intend to, manage the rest of her life alone. Two close friends her age, long deprived by divorce of their husbands, still hated to enter a crowded room unaccompanied. And beyond mere social gloss was the love she knew she felt for him. She didn't feel it now.

'Your problem,' he said from the far end of the room, 'is that you never think you have to explain yourself. You've gone from me. It must have occurred to you that I've noticed and that I mind. Just about bearable, I suppose, if I thought it wasn't going to last, or I knew the reason why. So . . . '

He was starting to come towards her at this point, but she never learned his conclusion, or let her rising irritation form a response, for at that moment, the phone rang. Automatically, she picked up the receiver. She was on duty, and sure enough, it was her clerk, Nigel Pauling. As ever, the voice was hesitant, on the edge of a stutter. But he was always efficient, pleasingly distant.

'I'm sorry to disturb you this late, My Lady.'

'It's all right. Go ahead.'

'We've had a call from counsel representing the Edith Cavell hospital, Wandsworth. They urgently need to transfuse a cancer patient, a boy of seventeen years. He and his parents are refusing consent. The hospital would like — '

'Why are they refusing?'

'Jehovah's Witnesses, My Lady.'

'Right.'

'The hospital's looking for an order that it will be lawful to proceed against their wishes.'

She looked at her watch. Just past ten thirty.

'How long have we got?'

'After Wednesday it will be dangerous, they're saying. Extremely dangerous.'

She looked around her. Jack had already left the room. She said, 'Then list it for hearing on short notice at 2 p.m. on Tuesday. And give notice to the respondents. Direct the hospital to inform the parents. They'll have liberty to apply.

32

Have a guardian appointed for the boy with legal representation. Direct the hospital to serve evidence by 4 p.m. tomorrow. The treating oncologist should serve a witness statement.'

For a moment her mind blanked. She cleared her throat and continued. 'I'll want to know why blood products are necessary. And the parents should use their best endeavours to file their evidence by noon on Tuesday.'

'I'll do it straight away.'

She went to the window and stared across the square, where shapes of trees were turning solid black in the last of the slow June dusk. As yet, the yellow street lamps illuminated no more than their circles of pavement. The Sunday-evening traffic was sparse now and barely a sound reached her from Gray's Inn Road or High Holborn. Only the tap of thinned-out raindrops on leaves and a distant musical gurgling from a nearby drainpipe. She watched a neighbour's cat down below pick a fastidious route around a puddle and dissolve into the darkness beneath a shrub. It didn't trouble her, Jack's withdrawal. Their exchange had been heading towards excruciating frankness. No denying the relief at being delivered onto the neutral ground, the treeless heath, of other people's problems. Religion again. It had its consolations. Since the boy was almost eighteen, the legal age of autonomy, his wishes would be a central concern.

Perhaps it was perverse to discover in this sudden interruption a promise of freedom. On the other side of the city a teenager confronted death for his own or his parents' beliefs. It was not her business or mission to save him, but to decide what was reasonable and lawful. She would have liked to see this boy for herself, remove herself from a domestic morass, as well as from the courtroom, for an hour or two, take a journey, immerse herself in the intricacies, fashion a judgment formed by her own observations. The parents' beliefs might be an affirmation of their son's, or a death sentence he dared not challenge. These days, finding out for yourself was highly unconventional. Back in the 1980s a judge could still have made the teenager a ward of court and seen him in chambers or hospital or at home. Back then, a noble ideal had somehow survived into the modern era, dented and rusty like a suit of armour. Judges had stood in for the monarch and had been for centuries the guardians of the nation's children. Nowadays, social workers from Cafcass did the job and reported back. The old system, slow and inefficient, preserved the human touch. Now, fewer delays, more boxes to tick, more to be taken on trust. The lives of children were held in computer memory, accurately, but rather less kindly.

Visiting the hospital was a sentimental whim. She dismissed the idea as she turned from the window to go back to her couch. She sat down with an impatient sigh and took up her judgment in the matter of the Jewish girls from Stamford Hill and their contested well-being. Her last pages, her conclusion, were again in her hands. But for the moment she couldn't bring herself to look at her own prose. This was not the first time that the absurdity and pointlessness of her involvement in a case had temporarily disabled her. Parents choosing a school for their children — an innocent, important, humdrum, private affair which a lethal blend of bitter division and too much money had transmuted into a monstrous clerical task, into box-files of legal documents so numerous and heavy they were hauled to court on trolleys, into hours of educated wrangling, procedural hearings, deferred decisions, the whole circus rising, but so slowly, through the judicial hierarchy like a lopsided, ill-tethered hot-air balloon. If the parents could not agree, the law, reluctantly, must take the decisions. Fiona would preside with all the seriousness and obedience to process of a nuclear scientist. Preside over what had begun with love and ended in loathing. The whole business should have been handed to a social worker, who could have taken half an hour to reach a sensible decision.

Fiona had found in favour of Judith, the fidgety ginger woman who, the clerk reported, at every break would dash across the marbled floors and through the polished stone arches of the Courts of Justice and out into the Strand to get to her next cigarette. The children should continue to attend the mixed school chosen for them by their mother. They could stay on until they were eighteen and have tertiary education if they so chose. The judgment paid respect to the Chareidi community, the continuity of its venerable traditions and observances, adding that the court took no view of its particular beliefs beyond noting that they were clearly sincerely held. However, witnesses from that community called by the father had helped undo his case. One respected figure had said, perhaps too proudly, that Chareidi women were expected to devote themselves to making a 'secure home' and that education past sixteen was not relevant. Another said it was highly unusual even for boys to enter the professions. A third had been a little too emphatic in his view that girls and boys should be kept well apart at school in order to maintain their purity. All this, Fiona had written, lay well outside mainstream parental practice and the generally held view that children should be encouraged in their aspirations. This must also be the view of the judicial reasonable parent. She accepted the social worker's opinion that if the girls were to be returned to the closed society of the father, they would be cut off from their mother. The reverse was less likely to be the case.

Above all, the duty of the court was to enable the children to come to adulthood and make their own decisions about the sort of life they wanted to lead. The girls might opt for their father's or their mother's version of religion, or they might find satisfaction in life elsewhere. Past eighteen they would be beyond the reach of parents and court. In parting, Fiona lightly rapped the paternal knuckles when she observed that Mr Bernstein had availed himself of female counsel and solicitor, and benefited from the experience of the court-appointed social worker, the astute and disorganised Cafcass lady. And he was implicitly bound to the order of a female judge. He should ask himself why he would deny his daughters the opportunity of a profession.

It was done. The corrections would be typed into her final draft early tomorrow morning. She stood and stretched, then picked up the whisky glasses and went to the kitchen to wash them. The warm water flowing over her hands was soothing and held her at the sink for a blank minute or so. But she was also listening out for Jack. The rumble of the ancient plumbing would let her know if he was preparing for bed. She went back into the sitting room to turn out the lights and found herself drawn again to her position at the window.

Down in the square, not far from the puddle that the cat had stepped around, her husband was towing a suitcase. Supported by a strap from his shoulder was the briefcase he used for work. He reached his car, their car, opened it, put his luggage on the back seat, got in and started the engine. As the headlights came on and the front wheels turned at full lock so that he could manoeuvre out of a tight parking space, she heard faintly the sound of the car radio. Pop music. But he hated pop music.

He must have packed his bag earlier in the evening, well before the start of their conversation. Or conceivably, halfway, when he had retreated to the bedroom. Instead of turmoil or anger or sorrow she felt only weariness. She thought she would be practical. If she could get to bed now she could avoid taking a sleeping pill. She went back into the kitchen, telling herself that she was not looking for a note on the pine table, where they always left each other notes.

There was nothing. She locked the front door and switched off the hallway lights. The bedroom looked undisturbed. She slid open his wardrobe and with a wifely eye calculated that he had taken three jackets, the newest of which was off-white linen from Gieves & Hawkes. In the bathroom she resisted opening his cabinet to estimate the contents of his washbag. She knew enough. In bed her only sensible thought was that he must have taken great care going along the hall without her hearing, and closed the front door inch by deceitful inch.

Even that was not enough to stop her descent into sleep. But sleep was no deliverance, for within the hour she was ringed by accusers. Or they were asking for help. The faces merged and separated. The baby twin, Matthew, with the earless bloated head and heart that wouldn't squeeze, simply stared, as he had on other nights. The sisters, Rachel and Nora, were calling to her in regretful tones, listing faults that may have been hers or their own. Jack was coming closer, pushing his newly creased forehead into her shoulder, explaining in a whining voice that her duty was to expand his choices into the future.

When her alarm rang at six thirty she sat up suddenly and for a moment stared without comprehension at the empty side of the bed. Then she went into the bathroom and began to prepare herself for a day in court.

2

She set off on her usual route from Gray's Inn Square to the Royal Courts of Justice and did her best not to think. In one hand she carried her briefcase, in the other, an umbrella aloft. The light was gloomy green and the city air was cool against her cheeks. She went out by the main entrance, avoiding small talk by nodding briskly at John, the friendly porter. Her hope was that she didn't look too much like a woman in crisis. She kept her mind off her situation by playing to her inner ear a piece she had learned by heart. Above the rush-hour din it was her ideal self she heard, the pianist she could never become, performing faultlessly Bach's second partita.

Rain had fallen most days of the summer, the city trees appeared swollen, their crests enlarged, the pavements were cleansed and smooth, the cars on High Holborn showroom clean. Last time she had looked, the Thames at high tide was also swollen and a darker brown, sullen and rebellious as it rose against the piers of the bridges, ready to take to the streets. But everyone pushed on, complaining, resolute, drenched. The jet stream was broken, bent southwards by factors beyond control, blocking the summer balm from the Azores, sucking in freezing air from the north. The consequence of man-made climate change, of melting sea ice disturbing the upper air, or irregular sunspot activity that was no one's fault, or natural variability, ancient rhythms, the planet's lot. Or all three, or any two. But what good were explanations and theories so early in the day? Fiona and the rest of London had work to get to.

By the time she was crossing the street to go down Chancery Lane, the rain was coming down harder, at a fair slant, driven by a sudden cold wind. Now it was darker, droplets bounced icily against her legs, crowds hurried by, silent, self-absorbed. Traffic along High Holborn poured past her, loud and vigorously undeterred, headlights gleaming on the asphalt while she listened again to the grand opening, the adagio in the Italian style, a distant promise of jazz in the slow dense chords. But there was no escape, the piece led her straight to Jack, for she had learned it as a birthday present to him last April. Dusk in the square, both just back from work, table lamps lit, a glass of champagne in his hand, her glass on the piano as she performed what she had patiently committed to memory in the previous weeks. Then his exclamations of recognition and delight and kindly overdone amazement at such a feat of recall, their long kiss at the end, her murmur of happy birthday, his moist eyes, the clink of their cut-glass flutes.

Thus the engine of self-pity began to turn and she helplessly summoned various treats she'd arranged for him. The list was unhealthily long — surprise operas, trips to Paris and Dubrovnik, Vienna, Trieste, Keith Jarrett in Rome (Jack, knowing nothing, instructed to pack a small case and passport and meet her at the airport straight from work), tooled cowboy boots, engraved hip flask and, in recognition of his new passion for geology, a nineteenth-century explorer's specimen hammer in a leather case. To bless his second adolescence on turning fifty, a trumpet that had once belonged to Guy Barker. These offerings represented only a fraction of the happiness she urged on him, and sex was only one part of that fraction, and only latterly a failure, elevated by him into a mighty injustice.

Sorrow and the mounting details of grievances, while her true anger lay ahead. An abandoned fifty-nine-year-old woman, in the infancy of old age, just learning to crawl. She forced herself back to her partita as she turned off Chancery Lane down the narrow passage that led her into Lincoln's Inn and its tangle of architectural splendour. Over the drumming of raindrops on her umbrella, she heard the lilting andante, walking pace, a rare marking in Bach, a beautiful carefree air over a strolling bass, her own steps falling in with the unearthly light-hearted melody as she went by Great Hall. The notes strained at some clear human meaning, but they meant nothing at all. Just loveliness, purified. Or love in its vaguest, largest form, for all people, indiscriminately. For children perhaps. Johann Sebastian had twenty by two marriages. He didn't let his work prevent him loving and teaching, caring and composing for those who survived. Children. The inevitable thought recurred as she moved on to the demanding fugue she had mastered, for love of her husband, and played at full tilt without fumbling, without failing to separate the voices.

Yes, her childlessness was a fugue in itself, a flight — this was the habitual theme she was trying now to resist — a flight from her proper destiny. Her failure to become a woman, as her mother understood the term. How she arrived at her state was a slow-patterned counterpoint played out with Jack over two decades, dissonances appearing then retreating, always reintroduced by her in moments of alarm, even horror, as the fertile years slipped by until they were gone, and she was almost too busy to notice.

A story best told at speed. After finals, more exams, then the call to the Bar, pupillage, a lucky invitation to prestigious chambers, some early success defending hopeless cases — how sensible it had seemed, to delay a child until her early thirties. And when those years came, they brought complex worthwhile cases, more success. Jack was also hesitant, arguing for holding back another year or two. Mid thirties then, when he was teaching in Pittsburgh and she worked a fourteen-hour day, drifting deeper into family law as the idea of her own family receded, despite the visits of nephews and nieces. In the following years, the first rumours that she might be elected precociously to the bench and required to be on circuit. But the call didn't come, not yet. And in her forties, there sprang up anxieties about elderly gravids and autism. Soon after, more young visitors to Gray's Inn Square, noisy demanding great-nephews, great-nieces, reminded her how hard it would be to squeeze an infant into her kind of life. Then rueful thoughts of adoption, some tentative enquiries — and throughout the accelerating years that followed, occasional agonies of doubt, firm late-night decisions concerning surrogate mothers undone in the early-morning rush to work. And when at last, at nine thirty one morning at the Royal Courts of Justice, she was sworn in by the Lord Chief Justice and took her oath of allegiance and her Judicial Oath before two hundred of her bewigged colleagues, and she stood proudly before them in her robes, the subject of a witty speech, she knew the game was up, she belonged to the law as some women had once been brides of Christ.

She crossed New Square and approached Wildy's bookshop. The music in her head had faded, but now came another old theme: self-blame. She was selfish, crabbed, drily ambitious. Pursuing her own ends, pretending to herself that her career was not in essence self-gratification, denying an existence to two or three warm and talented individuals. Had her children lived, it would have been shocking to think they might not have. And so here was her punishment, to face this disaster alone, without sensible grown-up children, concerned and phoning, downing tools and rallying round for urgent kitchen-table conferences, talking sense to their stupid father, bringing him back. But would she take him in? They would also need to talk sense to her. The almost existing children, the husky-voiced daughter, a museum curator perhaps, and the gifted less-settled son, good at too many things, who failed to complete his university course, but a far better pianist than

her. Both always affectionate, brilliant at Christmases and summer-holiday castles and entertaining
their youngest relations.

She walked along the passage past Wildy's,
untempted by the law books in the window
display, crossed Carey Street and went in the
rear entrance of the Courts of Justice. Down one
vaulted corridor, down another, up a flight of
stairs, past some courtrooms, down again, across
a courtyard, pausing at the foot of a staircase to
shake out her umbrella. The air always reminded
her of school, of the smell or feel of cold damp
stone and a faint thrill of fear and excitement.
She took the stairs rather than the lift,
heavy-footed on the red carpet as she turned
right towards her broad landing onto which the
doors of many High Court judges faced — like
an advent calendar, she sometimes thought. In
each broad and bookish room, her colleagues
would lose themselves daily in their cases, their
trials, in a labyrinth of detail and dissent against
which only a certain style of banter and irony
offered some protection. Most of the judges she
knew cultivated an elaborate sense of humour,
but this morning there was no one around
wanting to amuse her and she was glad. She was
probably first in. Nothing like a domestic storm
to toss you from your bed.

She paused in her doorway. Nigel Pauling,
correct and hesitant, was stooped over her desk,
setting out documents. There followed, as always
on a Monday, the ritual exchange of enquiries
into each other's weekends. Hers was 'quiet', and
saying that word she handed him the corrected

draft of the Bernstein judgment.

The day's business. In the Moroccan case, listed for ten o'clock, it was confirmed that the little girl had been removed from the jurisdiction to Rabat by the father, despite his undertakings to the court, and no word of her whereabouts, no word from the father, and his counsel at a loss. The mother was receiving psychiatric help, but would be in court. The intention was to apply through the Hague Convention, Morocco, by good fortune, being the one Islamic state to have signed up. All this was spoken in an apologetic hurry by Pauling, running a nervous hand through his hair, as though he were the abductor's brother. That poor pale woman, an underweight university don, who trembled while she sat in court, specialist in the sagas of Bhutan, devoted to her only child. And the father devoted too in his devious fashion, delivering his daughter from the evils of the unfaithful West. The papers were waiting on her desk.

The rest of the day's business was already clear in her mind. As she went to her desk she asked after the Jehovah's Witness case. The parents would be making an emergency application for legal aid and a certificate would be issued in the afternoon. The boy, the clerk told her, was suffering from a rare form of leukaemia.

'Let's give him a name.' She said it crisply and her tone surprised her.

When under pressure from her Pauling was always smoother, even a touch satirical. Now he gave her more information than she needed.

'Of course, My Lady. Adam. Adam Henry, an

only child. The parents are Kevin and Naomi. Mr Henry runs a small company. Groundwork, land drainage, that sort of thing. Apparently a virtuoso with the mechanical digger.'

After twenty minutes at her desk she went back across the landing, along a corridor to an alcove housing the coffee machine, with a glass image of hyper-real roasted beans spilling from a beaker, lit from the inside, brown and cream, as vivid in the gloom of the recess as an illuminated manuscript. A cappuccino with an extra shot, perhaps two. Better to start drinking it right here, where, undisturbed, she could nauseously picture Jack rising about now from an unfamiliar bed to prepare for work, the form beside him half asleep, well served in the small hours, stirring between sticky sheets, murmuring his name, calling him back. On a furious impulse, she pulled out her phone, scrolled through the numbers to their locksmith on the Gray's Inn Road, gave her four-digit PIN, then instructions for a change of lock. Of course, madam, right away. They held details of the existing lock. New keys to be delivered to the Strand today and nowhere else. Then, proceeding rapidly, hot plastic cup in her free hand, fearful of changing her mind, she called the Deputy Director of Estates, a gruff good-natured fellow, to let him know to expect a locksmith. So, she was bad, and feeling good about being bad. There must be a price for leaving her and here it was, to be in exile, a supplicant to his previous life. She would not permit him the luxury of two addresses.

Coming back along the corridor with her cup,

46

she was already wondering at her ridiculous transgression, obstructing her husband from rightful access, one of the clichés of marital breakdown, one that an instructing solicitor would advise a client — generally the wife — against in the absence of a court order. A professional life spent above the affray, advising then judging, loftily commenting in private on the viciousness and absurdity of divorcing couples, and now she was down there with the rest, swimming with the desolate tide.

These thoughts were suddenly interrupted. As she turned onto the wide landing she saw Mr Justice Sherwood Runcie framed in his doorway, waiting for her, grinning, rubbing his hands in parody of a stage villain to indicate he had something for her. He was a connoisseur of the latest word around the courts, which was usually accurate, and he took pleasure in passing it on. He was one of the few, perhaps the only colleague, she preferred to avoid, and not because he was unlikeable. He was, in fact, a charming man, who gave all his spare hours to a charity he had founded long ago in Ethiopia. But for Fiona he was an embarrassment by association. He had tried a murder case four years back, still awful to contemplate, and painful to remain silent about, as she must. And this in a brave little world, a village, where they routinely forgave each other their mistakes, where all suffered from time to time a judgment rudely overturned in the Court of Appeal, wrists slapped on points of law. But here was one of the greatest miscarriages of justice in modern times. And Sherwood! So untypically

gullible in the presence of a mathematically igno-
rant expert witness, then, to widespread disbelief
and horror, sending down an innocent bereaved
mother for the killing of her children, to be
bullied and assaulted by fellow inmates, demo-
nised by the tabloids, and have her first appeal
rejected. And when at last released, as she surely
had to be, to fall victim to drink, of which she
died.

The strange logic that drove this tragedy
could still keep Fiona awake at night. The
chances of a child dying from Sudden Infant
Death Syndrome were said in court to be nine
thousand to one. Therefore, the prosecution's
expert pronounced, the chances of two siblings
dying was this figure multiplied by itself. One in
eighty-one million. Almost impossible, and so
the mother must have had a hand in the deaths.
The world beyond the court was astonished. If
the cause of the syndrome was genetic, the
children shared a cause. If it was environmental,
they shared that too. If it was both, they shared
both. And what, by comparison, were the
chances of two babies from a stable middle-class
family being murdered by their mother? But
outraged probability theorists, statisticians and
epidemiologists were powerless to intervene.

In moments of disillusion with due process,
she only needed to summon the case of Martha
Longman and Runcie's lapse to confirm a
passing sense that the law, however much Fiona
loved it, was at its worst not an ass but a snake,
a poisonous snake. Unhelpfully, Jack took an
interest in the case and when it suited him, when

things weren't well between them, loudly loathed her profession and her implication in it, as if she herself had written the judgment.

But who could defend the judiciary once Longman's first appeal was rejected? The case was a sham from its inception. The pathologist, so it turned out, unaccountably withheld crucial evidence about an aggressive bacterial infection in the second child. The police and Crown Prosecution Service were illogically keen for a conviction, the medical profession was dishonoured by the evidence of its representative, and the entire system, this careless mob of professionals, drove a kindly woman, a well-regarded architect, towards persecution, despair and death. In the face of conflicting evidence from several expert medical witnesses about the causes of the infants' deaths, the law stupidly preferred a guilty verdict over scepticism and uncertainty. Runcie was, everyone agreed, an extremely nice fellow, and, the record showed, a good hard-working judge. But when Fiona heard that both the pathologist and the doctor were back at work, she couldn't help herself. The case turned her stomach.

Runcie was raising a hand in greeting and there was no choice but to stop in front of him and be affable.

'My dear.'

'Good morning, Sherwood.'

'I read a wonderful little exchange in Stephen Sedley's new book. Just your thing. It's from a Massachusetts trial. A rather insistent cross-examiner asks a pathologist whether he can be absolutely sure that a certain patient was dead before he began the autopsy. The pathologist says he's absolutely certain. Oh, but how can you be so sure? Because, the pathologist says, his brain was in a jar sitting on my desk. But, says the cross-examiner, could the patient still have been alive nevertheless? Well, comes the answer, it's possible he could have been alive and practising law somewhere.'

Even as Runcie exploded into hilarity at his own story, his eyes were fixed on hers, gauging whether her mirth would match his own. She did her best. Jokes against the legal profession were what the legal profession loved most.

At last, installed behind her desk with her now lukewarm coffee, contemplating the matter of a child removed from the jurisdiction. She pretended not to notice Pauling on the other side of the room as he cleared his throat to say something then thought better of it and vanished. At some point, her own concerns also vanished as she forced her attention on the submissions, and began reading at speed.

The court rose to her on the stroke of ten. She listened to counsel for the distressed mother, applying to retrieve her child through the Hague Convention. When the Moroccan husband's counsel got to his feet to persuade Fiona of some ambiguity in his client's undertaking, she cut him off.

'I was expecting to find you blushing on behalf of your client, Mr Soames.'

The matter was technical, absorbing. The thin frame of the mother remained partly hidden behind counsel, and seemed to shrink further as the arguments became more abstract. It was likely that when the court rose, Fiona would never see her again. The sad affair would come before a Moroccan judge.

Next, she heard an urgent application on behalf of a wife seeking maintenance pending suit. The judge listened, she asked questions, she granted the application. At lunch-time she wanted to be alone. Pauling brought her sandwiches and a bar of chocolate to eat at her desk. Her phone lay under some papers, and at last she gave in, scanned the screen for texts or missed calls. Nothing. She told herself she felt neither disappointment nor relief. She drank tea and allowed herself ten minutes to read the newspapers. Mostly Syria, reports and lurid photographs: the government shelling civilians, refugees on the road, impotent condemnations from foreign ministries around the world, an eight-year-old boy on a bed, left foot amputated, weak-chinned etiolated Assad shaking hands with a Russian official, rumours of nerve gas.

There was far greater misery elsewhere, but after lunch she confronted more of the local kind. She was dismissive of an ex *parte* application for an order excluding a husband from the matrimonial home. The presentation was protracted, the owlish counsel's nervous blink irritated her further.

'Why are you doing this without notice? I see nothing in the papers that would make that necessary. What communication have you tried to have with the other side? None, as far as I can see. If the husband's happy to give an undertaking to your client, you really shouldn't be bothering me with this. If he isn't then serve notice and I'll hear both sides.'

The court rose, she stalked out. Then back to hear argument for and against a prohibitive-steps order on behalf of a man who said he feared violence from his ex-wife's boyfriend. Much legal argument about the boyfriend's prison record, but it concerned fraud, not assault, and finally she refused the application. An undertaking would have to do. A cup of tea in her room, then back again to hear a divorcing mother's emergency application for her three children to have their passports lodged with the court. Fiona was minded to grant it, but after she heard argument about the aggravating complication that would follow, she refused.

Back in her room at five forty-five. She sat at her desk, staring blankly at her bookshelves. When Pauling came in, she started, and thought she may have been asleep. He let her know that press interest in the Jehovah's Witness case was now strong. Most of tomorrow morning's papers would carry the story. On the press websites there were pictures of the boy with his family. The parents themselves may have been the source, or a relative grateful for some quick cash. The clerk put in Fiona's hands the papers for the case and a brown envelope which clinked mysteriously as she unsealed it. A letter bomb from a disappointed plaintiff? It had happened before, when a device, clumsily assembled by an enraged husband, failed to explode in the face of her then clerk. But yes, her new keys, opening the way to her other life, her transformed existence.

And so, half an hour later, she set off towards it, but by a circuitous route, for she was reluctant to enter the empty apartment. She left by the main entrance and walked west on the Strand to the Aldwych, then went north along Kingsway. The sky was battleship grey, the rain barely noticeable, the Monday rush-hour crowds lighter than usual. In prospect, another one of those too long, dim summer evenings of low cloud. Total darkness would have suited her better. When she passed a key-cutting shop, she made her heart beat harder imagining a shouting row with Jack about the lock-out, face to face in the square under the dripping trees, overheard by neighbours, who were also colleagues. She would be entirely in the wrong.

She turned east, passed the LSE, skirted Lincoln's Inn Fields, crossed High Holborn, then, to delay her arrival home, went west again, down narrow streets of mid-Victorian artisanal workshops, now hairdressers, lock-ups, sandwich bars. She crossed Red Lion Square, past empty wet aluminium chairs and tables of the park café, past Conway Hall where a small crowd was gathered waiting to go in, decent, white-haired, careworn people, Quakers perhaps, ready for an evening of remonstration with things as they stood. Well, she had her own such evening ahead. But to belong to the law and all its historical accumulation bound one closer to things as they stood. Even as you resisted or denied it. More than half a dozen embossed invitation cards lay on a polished walnut table in the hallway at Gray's Inn Square. The Inns of Court, the universities, charities, various royal societies, eminent acquaintances, calling on Jack and Fiona Maye, themselves crafted through the years into a miniature institution, to step out in public in their best clothes, lend their weight, eat, drink, talk, and return home before midnight.

She went slowly along Theobald's Road, still holding off the moment of her return, wondering again whether it was not love she had lost so much as a modern form of respectability, whether it was not contempt and ostracism she feared, as in the novels of Flaubert and Tolstoy, but pity. To be the object of general pity was also a form of social death. The nineteenth century was closer than most women thought. To be caught out enacting her part in a cliché showed poor taste rather than a moral lapse. Restless husband in one last throw, brave wife maintaining her dignity, younger woman remote and blameless. And she had thought her acting days ended on a summer lawn, just before she fell in love.

As it turned out, coming home was not so difficult after all. She was occasionally back from work before Jack, and it surprised her to feel soothed as she stepped into the sanctuary dimness of the hall and its scent of lavender polish, and half pretend to herself that nothing had changed, or that it was about to come right. Before she turned on the lights she put her bag down and listened. The summer cold had brought on the central heating. Now the radiators ticked unevenly as they cooled. She heard the faint sound of orchestral music from a downstairs apartment, Mahler, *langsam und ruhig*. Less faintly, a song thrush pedantically repeating each ornamental phrase, the sound conducted cleanly down a chimney flue. Then she went through the rooms, turning on the lights, even though it was barely seven thirty. Back in the hall to retrieve her bag, she noticed that the locksmith had left no trace of his visit. Not even a wood shaving. Why should he, when he was only changing the barrel of the lock, and why should she care? But the absence of any trace of his visit was a reminder of Jack's absence, a little tug downwards on her spirits and to counter it she took her papers into the kitchen and skimmed through one of the next day's cases while she waited for the kettle to boil.

She could have phoned one of three friends, but she could not bear to hear herself explain her situation and make it irreversibly real. Too soon for sympathy or advice, too soon to hear Jack damned by loyal chums. Instead, she passed the evening in an empty state, a condition of numbness. She ate bread, cheese and olives with a glass of white wine, and passed an interminable period at the piano. First, in a spirit of defiance, she played through her Bach partita. Occasionally, she and a barrister, Mark Berner, performed songs, and she had seen that afternoon that he was listed for tomorrow to represent the hospital in the Jehovah's Witness case. The next concert was many months ahead, just before Christmas, in the Great Hall in Gray's Inn, and they had yet to agree a programme. But they had a few encore pieces off by heart and she played through them now, imagining the tenor's part, lingering over Schubert's mournful 'Der Leiermann', the hurdy-gurdy man, who is poor and wretched and ignored. Such concentration protected her from thoughts, and she had no sense of passing time. When she rose at last from the piano stool, her knees and hips were stiff. In the bathroom she bit into half of a sleeping pill, stared at the ragged remainder in her palm, then swallowed that too.

Twenty minutes later she lay in her half of the bed listening through closed eyes to the radio news, the shipping forecast, the national anthem, then the World Service. As she waited for oblivion, she heard the news again and perhaps a third time, then calm voices discussing the day's savagery — suicide bombers in crowded public places in Pakistan and Iraq, shelling of apartment blocks in Syria, Islam's war with itself conducted by means of twisted car frames and rubble, and body parts flung across marketplaces, and ordinary people wailing in shock and grief. Then the voices turned to discuss American drones over Waziristan, last week's bloody assault on a wedding party. While the reasonable voices pressed on into the night, she curled up for a troubled sleep.

★　★　★

The morning passed like a hundred others. Applications, submissions rapidly assimilated, argument heard, judgments delivered, orders dispensed, and Fiona moving between her room and the court, bumping into colleagues on the way, something even festive in their quick exchanges, the clerk's weary call of 'Court rise', her minimal nod towards the opening barrister, her occasional weak joke fawningly received by counsel for both sides with little attempt to conceal their insincerity, and the litigants, if they were a divorcing couple, as they all were this Tuesday morning, seated well apart behind their representation, in no mood to smile.

And her mood? She counted herself reasonably adept at monitoring it, naming it, and she detected a significant shift. Yesterday, she now decided, she had been in shock, in an unreal state of acceptance, prepared to tell herself that she had, at worst, to endure the commiseration of family and friends and a degree of severe social inconvenience — those embossed invitations she must refuse while hoping to conceal her embarrassment. This morning, waking with a cold part of a bed to her left — a form of amputation — she felt the first conventional ache of abandonment. She thought of Jack at his best and longed for him, the hairy bony hardness of his shins, down which, half asleep, she would let the soft underside of her foot slide at the alarm clock's first assault, when she would roll onto his outstretched arm and wait and doze beneath the duvet's warmth, face into his chest, until the clock's second call. That naked childlike surrender, before she rose to assume an adult's armour, seemed first thing this morning like an essential from which she was banished. When she stood in the bathroom, when she stepped out of her pyjamas, her body looked foolish in the full-length mirror. Miraculously shrunken in some parts, bloated in others. Bottom heavy. A ridiculous package. Fragile, This Way Up. Why would anyone not leave her?

Washing, dressing, drinking coffee, leaving a note and arranging a new key for the cleaning lady, brought these raw feelings under control. And so she began her morning, looked for her husband in emails, texts and post, found nothing, gathered her papers, her umbrella and her phone, and walked to work. His silence appeared ruthless and it shocked her. She knew only that Melanie, the statistician, lived somewhere near Muswell Hill. Not impossible, to track her down, or look for Jack at the university. But what humiliation then, to find him in a departmental corridor, walking towards her, arm in arm with his lover. Or to find him alone. What could she propose beyond a pointless, ignominious plea for his return? She could demand confirmation that he had left his marriage, and he would tell her what she already knew and didn't want to hear. So she would wait until a certain book or shirt or tennis racket drew him back to the locked apartment. Then it would be his task to search her out, and when they spoke, she would be on her own ground, dignity intact, outwardly at least.

It would not have been apparent, but her spirits were heavy as she set about Tuesday's list. The last case of the morning was prolonged by complex argument over commercial law. A divorcing husband claimed that the three million pounds he had been ordered to pay to his wife was not his to give away. It belonged to his company. It emerged, but far too slowly, that he was the sole director and only employee of an enterprise that made or did nothing — it was a fig leaf for a beneficial tax arrangement. Fiona found for the wife. The afternoon was now cleared for the hospital's emergency application in the Jehovah's Witness case. In her room once more, she ate a sandwich and an apple at her desk while she read through the submissions. Meanwhile, her colleagues were lunching splendidly at Lincoln's Inn. Forty minutes later, one clarifying thought accompanied her as she made her way to courtroom eight. Here was a matter of life and death.

She entered, the court rose, she sat and watched the parties below her settle. At her elbow was a slim pile of creamy white paper beside which she laid down her pen. It was only then, at the sight of these clean sheets, that the last traces, the stain, of her own situation vanished completely. She no longer had a private life, she was ready to be absorbed.

Ranged before her were the three parties. For the hospital, her friend Mark Berner QC, and two instructing solicitors. For Adam Henry and his guardian, the Cafcass officer, was an elderly barrister, John Tovey, not known to Fiona, and his instructing solicitor. For the parents, another silk, Leslie Grieve QC, and two solicitors. Sitting by them were Mr and Mrs Henry. He was a wiry, tanned man in a well-cut suit and tie in which he himself could have passed for a successful member of the judiciary. Mrs Henry was big-boned and wore outsized glasses with red frames that shrunk her eyes to points. She sat upright, with tightly folded arms. Neither parent looked particularly cowed. Outside in the corridors, Fiona assumed, journalists would soon be assembling to wait until she allowed them in to hear her decision.

She began. 'You're all aware that we are here on a matter of extreme urgency. Time is of the essence. Everyone please bear this in mind and speak briefly and to the point. Mr Berner.'

She inclined her head towards him and he stood. He was smoothly bald, bulky, but with dainty feet — size five, it was rumoured — for which he was mocked behind his back. His voice was a decent rich tenor and together their greatest moment had been last year when they performed Schubert's 'Der Erlkönig' at a Gray's Inn dinner for a retiring law lord with a passion for Goethe.

'I shall indeed be brief, My Lady, for, as you indicate, the situation is pressing. The applicant in the matter is the Edith Cavell General, Wandsworth, which is seeking the leave of this court to treat a boy, named A in the papers, who will be eighteen in less than three months. He experienced sharp stomach pains on the fourteenth of May when he was putting on his pads to open the batting for his school cricket team. During the following two days these pains became severe, unbearable even. The GP, despite great expertise and experience, was at a loss and referred — '

'I've read the papers, Mr Berner.'

The barrister moved on. 'Then, My Lady, I believe it is accepted by all parties that Adam is suffering from leukaemia. The hospital wishes to treat him in the usual manner with four drugs, a therapeutic procedure universally recognised and practised by haematologists, as I can show — '

'No need, Mr Berner.'

'Thank you, My Lady.'

Berner advanced quickly to outline the conventional course of treatment and this time Fiona did not intervene. Two of the four drugs targeted the leukaemia cells directly, whereas the other two poisoned much in their path, in particular the bone marrow, thereby compromising the body's immune system and its ability to make red and white blood cells and platelets. Consequently, it was usual to transfuse during treatment. In this case, however, the hospital was prevented from doing so. Adam and his parents were Jehovah's Witnesses and it was contrary to their faith to accept blood products into their bodies. This apart, the boy and his parents agreed to any treatment the hospital could offer.

'And what has been offered?'

'My Lady, in deference to the family's wishes, only the leukaemia-specific drugs have been administered. They are not considered sufficient. It's at this point I'd like to call the consultant haematologist.'

'Very well.'

Mr Rodney Carter took the stand and was sworn in. Tall, stooping, severe, thick white eyebrows from under which he glared with ferocious disdain. From the top pocket of his pale grey three-piece suit there protruded a blue silk handkerchief. He gave the impression that he

61

considered the court procedure a nonsense and that the boy should be dragged by the scruff of his neck to an immediate transfusion.

There followed standard questions to establish Carter's bona fides, his length of experience and seniority. When Fiona cleared her throat softly, Berner took the hint and pressed on. He asked the doctor to summarise for the benefit of the judge the patient's condition.

'Not at all good.'

He was asked to elaborate.

Carter drew breath and looked about him, saw the parents and looked away. His patient was weak, he said, and, as expected, showing the first signs of breathlessness. If he, Carter, had had a free hand in treatment, he would have expected an eighty to ninety per cent chance of a full remission. With the current course, the chances were much reduced.

Berner asked for specific data concerning Adam's blood.

When the boy was admitted, Carter said, the haemoglobin count was 8.3 grams per decilitre. The norm being around 12.5. It had declined steadily. Three days ago it had been 6.4. This morning it was at 4.5. If it dropped further to 3, the situation would be extremely dangerous.

Mark Berner was about to ask another question but Carter spoke over him.

'The white cell count is usually somewhere between 5 and 9. It's now 1.7. As for the plate-lets — '

Fiona interrupted. 'Would you kindly remind me of their function?'

'Necessary for clotting, My Lady.'

The norm, the consultant told the court, was 250. The boy's count was 34. Below 20 one would expect spontaneous bleeding to occur. At this point, Mr Carter turned his head a little away from the barrister so that he seemed to address the parents. 'The latest analysis,' he said gravely, 'shows us that no new blood is being produced. A healthy adolescent might be expected to produce five hundred billion blood cells a day.'

'And if, Mr Carter, you could transfuse?'

'The boy would stand a decent chance. Though not as good as it would have been if we'd transfused from the start.'

Berner paused briefly, and when he spoke again, he lowered his voice, as though to dramatise the possibility of Adam Henry overhearing him. 'Have you discussed with your patient what will happen to him if he is not transfused?'

'Only in the broadest terms. He knows he could die.'

'He has no idea of the manner of his death. Would you care to give the court an outline?'

'If you want.'

Berner and Carter appeared to be colluding in the grisly facts for the benefit of the parents. It was a reasonable line of approach and Fiona did not intervene.

Carter said slowly, 'It will be distressing, not only for himself but for the medical team treating him. Some of the staff are angry. They routinely hang blood, as the Americans put it, all day long. They simply can't understand why they should risk losing this patient. One feature of his

63

decline will be his fight to breathe, a fight he will find frightening and is bound to lose. The sensation will be one of drowning slowly. Before that he may suffer internal bleeding. Renal failure is a possibility. Some patients lose their sight. Or he may suffer a stroke, with any number of neurological consequences. Cases differ. The only sure thing is that it would be a horrible death.'

'Thank you, Mr Carter.'

Leslie Grieve for the parents rose to cross-examine. Fiona knew Grieve a little by reputation, but at that moment couldn't recall whether he had ever appeared before her. She had seen him about the law courts — somewhat foppish, with silver, centre-parted hair, high cheekbones, long thin nose, haughtily flared. There was a looseness or freedom of limb that was in agreeable contrast to the reined-in movements of his graver colleagues. The entire grand and gay effect was complicated by a problem he had with his vision, a squint of some sort, for he never appeared to be looking at what he was seeing. This disability added to his allure. It sometimes disoriented witnesses in cross-examination and it may have caused the doctor's tetchiness now.

Grieve said, 'You accept, do you not, Mr Carter, that the freedom of choice of medical treatment is a fundamental human right in adults?'

'I do.'

'And treatment without consent would constitute a trespass of the person, or indeed an assault of that person.'

'I agree.'

'And Adam is close to being an adult, as the

law defines it in such instances.'

Carter said, 'If his eighteenth birthday was tomorrow morning, he would not yet have attained his majority today.'

This was said with vehemence. Grieve was unruffled. 'Adam is very nearly an adult. Is it not the case that he has expressed his view to treatment intelligently and articulately?'

At this point, the consultant's stoop vanished and he grew another inch. 'His views are those of his parents. They're not his own. His objection to being transfused is based on the doctrines of a religious cult for which he may well become a pointless martyr.'

'Cult is a strong word, Mr Carter,' Grieve said quietly. 'Do you yourself have any religious belief?'

'I'm an Anglican.'

'Is the Church of England a cult?'

Fiona looked up from her note-taking. Grieve acknowledged her by pursing his lips and pausing on a long intake of breath. The doctor looked as if he was set to leave the stand, but the barrister had not finished with him.

'Are you aware, Mr Carter, that the World Health Organisation estimates that between fifteen and twenty per cent of new AIDS cases are caused by blood transfusions?'

'No such cases have occurred in my hospital.'

'The haemophiliac communities of various countries have suffered the tragedy of AIDS infection on a massive scale, have they not?'

'That was a good while ago and no longer happens.'

'And other infections are possible via transfusion, are they not? Hepatitis, Lyme disease, malaria, syphilis, Chagas disease, graft-versus-host disease, transfusion-related lung disease. And, of course, variant CJD.'

'All exceedingly rare.'

'But known to occur. And then there are haemolytic reactions due to mismatched blood groups.'

'Also rare.'

'Really? Let me quote to you, Mr Carter, from the highly respected *Manual for Blood Conservation*: "There are at least twenty-seven stages between taking a blood sample and the recipient receiving their transfusion and there is potential for error at each stage of the process."'

'Our staff are highly trained. They take great care. I don't recall a single haemolytic reaction in years.'

'If we added all these dangers up, wouldn't you say there was enough to give a rational person pause, Mr Carter, without that person being a member of what you call a cult?'

'These days, blood products are tested to the highest standards.'

'Nevertheless, it would not be wholly irrational to hesitate before accepting to be transfused.'

Carter thought for a moment. 'Hesitate, perhaps, at a stretch. But to refuse in a case like Adam's would be irrational.'

'You accept that hesitation is in order. So it wouldn't be unreasonable surely, given all the possibilities of infection and error, for the patient to insist that his consent be sought.'

The consultant made a show of self-control.

'You're playing with words. If I'm not permitted to transfuse this patient, he may not recover. At the very least he could lose his sight.'

Grieve said, 'Isn't there something like an ill-considered fashion in your profession for transfusion, given the risks? It's not evidence-based, is it, Mr Carter? It's rather like bloodletting in the old days, except, of course, in reverse. Patients who lose a third of a pint of blood during surgery are routinely transfused, no? And yet, a donor gives up a whole pint and goes straight back to work afterwards, and no harm done.'

'I can't comment on the clinical judgement of others. The general view, I suppose, is that a patient weakened by surgery should have all the blood that God allotted.'

'Isn't it the case that Jehovah's Witness patients are regularly treated now by what's called bloodless surgery? No transfusions are necessary. Allow me to quote to you from the *American Journal of Otolaryngology*: 'Bloodless surgery has come to represent good practice, and in the future it may well be the accepted standard of care.''

The consultant was dismissive. 'We're not talking of surgery here. This patient needs blood because his treatment prevents him from making his own. It's as simple as that.'

'Thank you, Mr Carter.'

Grieve sat down and John Tovey, who appeared to depend on a cane with a silver head and who was counsel for Adam Henry, breathily got to his feet to cross-examine the consultant.

'You've clearly spent time alone in conversation with Adam.'

'I have.'

'Have you formed an impression as to his intelligence?'

'Extremely intelligent.'

'Is he articulate?'

'Yes.'

'Is his judgement, his cognition, clouded by his medical condition?'

'Not as yet.'

'Have you suggested to him that he needs a transfusion?'

'I have.'

'And what has been his response?'

'He firmly refuses it on the grounds of his religion.'

'Are you aware of his exact age in years and months?'

'He's seventeen years and nine months.'

'Thank you, Mr Carter.'

Berner rose to re-examine.

'Mr Carter, will you remind me again how long you've specialised in haematology?'

'Twenty-seven years.'

'What are the risks of an adverse reaction to a blood transfusion?'

'Very low. Nothing compared to the certain damage that will be done in this case by failing to transfuse.'

Berner indicated that he had nothing more to ask.

Fiona said, 'In your opinion, Mr Carter, how much time do we have to resolve this matter?'

'If I can't give blood to this boy by tomorrow morning we'll be in very dangerous territory.'

Berner sat. Fiona thanked the doctor, who left with a curt, possibly resentful, nod towards the bench. Grieve got to his feet and said he would call the father straight away. When Mr Henry came to the stand, he asked if he might swear on the New World Translation. The clerk told him there was only the King James. Mr Henry nodded and swore on it, then settled his gaze patiently on Grieve.

Kevin Henry stood around five foot six and looked as lithe and strong as a trapeze artist. He may have been adept with a mechanical digger, but he looked equally at home in his well-cut grey suit and pale green silk tie. The drift of Leslie Grieve's questions was to draw from him a picture of early struggle, then the blossoming of a loving, stable and happy family. Who could doubt it? The Henrys had married young, at nineteen, seventeen years ago. The early years, when Kevin was employed as a labourer, were hard. He was 'a bit of a wild man', drank too much, was abusive to his wife, Naomi, though he never hit her. He was eventually sacked for being too often late for work. The rent was overdue, the baby cried through the night, the couple rowed, the neighbours complained. The Henrys were threatened with eviction from their one-bedroom flat in Streatham.

Deliverance came in the form of two polite young men from America who doorstepped Naomi one afternoon. They came back the next day and spoke to Kevin, who was hostile at first. Finally, a visit to the nearest Kingdom Hall, a kindly welcome and then, slowly, through meeting some nice people who soon became friends, and helpful talks with wise elders of the congregation, and then Bible study, which they found hard at first — slowly, order and peace came into their lives. Kevin and Naomi began to live in the truth. They learned of the future that God had in store for mankind and they fulfilled their duty by working to spread the word. They discovered that there would be a paradise on earth and they could be a part of it by belonging to that privileged group known to the Witnesses as 'other sheep'.

They began to understand the preciousness of life. As they became better parents, their son became calmer. Kevin went on a government-sponsored course to learn how to operate heavyweight machinery. Not long after he qualified he was offered a job. On their way to Kingdom Hall with Adam to give thanks, the couple told each other they had fallen in love all over again. They held hands in the street, something they had never done before. Since that time years ago, they had lived in the truth and raised Adam in the truth within the close, supportive network of their Witness friends. Five years ago, Kevin started his own company. He owned a few diggers, dumpers and a crane and employed nine men. Now God had visited leukaemia on their son and Kevin and Naomi confronted the ultimate test of faith.

To each of the barrister's prompting questions, Mr Henry gave a considered reply. He was respectful, but not in awe of the court the way many people were. He spoke plainly about his early failures, seemed unembarrassed to recall the hand-holding moment, didn't hesitate in this setting to use the word love. Frequently, he turned from Grieve's question to address Fiona directly and held her gaze. Automatically, she tried to place his accent. A touch of cockney, a fainter trace of West Country — the confident voice of a man who took his own competence for granted, well used to giving orders. Certain British jazzmen spoke this way, a tennis coach she knew, and non-commissioned officers, senior policemen, paramedics, an oil-rig foreman who had once come before her. Not men who ran the world, but who made it run.

Grieve paused to mark the end of this five-minute history then asked softly, 'Mr Henry, will you tell the court why Adam is refusing a blood transfusion.'

Mr Henry hesitated, as if to consider the question for the first time. He turned from Grieve to direct his answer at Fiona. 'You have to understand,' he said, 'that blood is the essence of what's human. It's the soul, it's life itself. And just as life is sacred, so is blood.' He seemed to have finished but then he added quickly, 'Blood stands for the gift of life that every living soul should be grateful for.' He delivered these sentences not as cherished beliefs but as statements of fact, like an engineer describing the construction of a bridge.

Grieve waited, conveying by his silence that his question had not been answered. But Kevin Henry was done and looked directly ahead.

Grieve prompted, 'So, if blood's a gift, why

71

would your son refuse it from the doctors?'

'Mixing your own blood with the blood of an animal or another human being is pollution, contamination. It's a rejection of the Creator's wonderful gift. That's why God specifically forbids it in Genesis and Leviticus and Acts.'

Grieve was nodding. Mr Henry added simply, 'The Bible is the word of God. Adam knows it must be obeyed.'

'Do you and your wife love your son, Mr Henry?'

'Yes. We love him.' He said it quietly and looked at Fiona with defiance.

'And if refusing a blood transfusion should cause his death?'

Again, Kevin Henry stared ahead at the wood-panelled wall. When he spoke his voice was tight. 'He'll take his place in the kingdom of heaven on earth that's to come.'

'And you and your wife. How will you feel?'

Naomi Henry still sat firmly upright, her expression behind her glasses impossible to read. She had turned to face the barrister rather than her husband in the witness stand. From where Fiona sat it was not clear if Mrs Henry's eyes, shrunken behind their lenses, were open.

Kevin Henry said, 'He'll have done what is right and true, what the Lord commanded.'

Once more, Grieve waited, then he said in a falling tone, 'You'll be grief-stricken, won't you, Mr Henry?'

At this point the contrived kindness in the counsel's tone caused the father's voice to fail. He could only nod. Fiona saw a ripple of muscle around his throat as he regained control.

The barrister said, 'Is this refusal Adam's decision, or is it really your own?'

'We couldn't turn him from it, even if we wanted to.'

For several minutes Grieve pursued this line of questioning, looking to establish that the boy was not unduly influenced. Two elders had visited the bedside on occasions. Mr Henry was not invited to be present. But afterwards, in a hospital corridor, the elders had told him that they had been impressed and moved by the boy's grasp of his situation and his knowledge of the scriptures. They were satisfied that he knew his own mind and that he was living, as he was prepared to die, in the truth.

Fiona sensed Berner was about to object. But he knew she would not waste time in discounting hearsay evidence.

A final set of questions from Leslie Grieve were prompts to allow Mr Henry to expound on the emotional maturity of his son. He did so proudly, nothing in his tone now to suggest that he thought he was about to lose him.

It was not until three thirty that Mark Berner rose to cross-examine. He began by expressing sympathy to Mr and Mrs Henry for the illness of their son and hopes for a complete recovery — a sure sign, to Fiona at least, that the barrister was about to cut up rough. Kevin Henry inclined his head.

'Just to start by clearing up a simple matter, Mr Henry. The books of the Bible you mention, Genesis, Leviticus and Acts, forbid you to *eat* blood or, in one case, exhort you to abstain from it. In the New World Translation of Genesis, for example, it says, 'Only flesh with its soul — its blood — you must not eat.''

'That's correct.'

'Nothing about transfusion then.'

Mr Henry said patiently, 'I think you'll find that in the Greek and the Hebrew the original has the meaning of 'take into the body'.'

'Very well. But at the time of these Iron Age texts, transfusion didn't exist. How could it be forbidden?'

Kevin Henry shook his head. There was pity or generous tolerance in his voice. 'It certainly existed in the mind of God. You need to understand that these books are his word. He inspired his chosen prophets to write down his will. It doesn't matter what age it was, Stone, Bronze or whatever.'

'That may well be, Mr Henry. But many Jehovah's Witnesses query this idea about transfusion on exactly these terms. They're prepared to accept blood products, or certain blood products, without rejecting their faith. Isn't it the case that other options are open to young Adam and you could play your part in persuading him to take them and save his life?'

Henry turned back towards Fiona. 'There are a very few who depart from the teachings of the Governing Body. I don't know anyone in our congregation, and our elders are quite clear about it.'

The overhead lights gleamed brilliantly on Berner's polished scalp. In virtual parody of the hectoring cross-examiner, he held the lapel of his jacket in his right hand. 'These strict elders have been visiting your son every day, have they not? They're keen to make sure he doesn't change his mind.'

The first hint of irritation afflicted Kevin Henry. He squared up to Berner, gripping the edge of the witness stand, leaning slightly forward, as though only an invisible leash restrained him. His tone, however, remained level. 'These are kind and decent men. Other churches have their priests going around the wards. My son gets advice and comfort from the elders. If he didn't he'd let me know.'

'Isn't it true that if he agreed to be transfused he'd be what you call disfellowshipped? In other words, cast out of the community?'

'Disassociated. But it isn't going to happen. He isn't going to change his mind.'

'He's technically still a child, Mr Henry, in your care. So it's your mind I want to change. He's frightened of being shunned, isn't that the term you use? Shunned for not doing what you and the elders want. The only world he knows would turn its back on him for preferring life to a terrible death. Is that a free choice for a young lad?'

Kevin Henry paused to think. For the first time he looked back at his wife. 'If you spent five minutes in his company you'd realise he's someone who knows what he's about and is able to make a decision according to his faith.'

'I rather think we'd find a terrified and seriously ill boy desperate for the approval of his parents. Mr Henry, have you told Adam that he's free to have a transfusion if he so wishes? And that you'd still love him?'

'I've told him that I love him.'

'Only that?'

'It's enough.'

'Do you know when Jehovah's Witnesses were commanded to refuse blood transfusions?'

'It's set down in Genesis. It dates from the Creation.'

'It dates from 1945, Mr Henry. Before then it was perfectly acceptable. Are you happy with a situation in which in modern times a committee in Brooklyn has decided your son's fate?'

Kevin Henry lowered his voice, out of respect for the subject matter perhaps, or in the face of a difficult matter. Again he included Fiona in his answer, and there was warmth in his voice. 'The Holy Spirit guides the anointed representatives — we call them the slaves, Your Honour — it helps them towards deep truths that weren't previously understood.' He turned back to Berner and said matter-of-factly, 'The Governing Body is Jehovah's channel of communication to us. It's his voice. If there are changes in the teaching it's because God only gradually reveals his purpose.'

'This voice doesn't tolerate much dissent. It's says here in this copy of *The Watchtower* that independent thinking was promoted by Satan at the beginning of his rebellion in October 1914 and such thinking should be avoided by followers. Is this what you're telling Adam, Mr Henry? That he must watch out for Satan's influence?'

'We like to avoid dissent and quarrels and keep

76

ourselves unified.' Mr Henry's confidence was growing. He appeared to address the barrister privately. 'You probably have no idea what it is to submit to a higher authority. You need to understand that we do so of our own free will.'

There was a trace of a lopsided smile on Mark Berner's face. Admiration for his adversary, perhaps. 'You've just told my learned colleague that in your twenties your life was a mess. You said you were a bit of a wild man. Hardly likely, is it, Mr Henry, that several years earlier, when you were Adam's age, you knew your own mind.'

'He's lived his whole life in the truth. I didn't have that privilege.'

'And then, as I recall, you said you discovered that life was precious. Did you mean other people's lives or just your own?'

'All life is the gift of the Lord. And his to take away.'

'Easy to say, Mr Henry, when it's not your life.'

'Harder to say when it's your own son.'

'Adam writes poetry. Do you approve of that?'

'I don't think it's particularly relevant to his life.'

'You've rowed with him about it, haven't you?'

'We've had serious conversations.'

'Is masturbation a sin, Mr Henry?'

'Yes.'

'And abortion? Homosexuality?'

'Yes.'

'And this is what Adam has been taught to believe?'

'It's what he knows to be true.'

'Thank you, Mr Henry.'

John Tovey rose and, somewhat breathlessly, told Fiona that given the hour he had no questions to ask of Mr Henry, but he would call the social worker, the Cafcass officer. Marina Greene was slight, sandy-haired and spoke in short precise sentences. Helpful, at this stage of the afternoon. Adam, she said, was highly intelligent. He knew his Bible. He knew the arguments. He said he was prepared to die for his faith.

He had said the following — and here, with the judge's permission, Marina Greene read from her notebook. 'I'm my own man. I'm separate from my parents. Whatever my parents' ideas are, I'm deciding for myself.'

Fiona asked what action Mrs Greene thought the court should take. She said her view was simple, and she apologised for not knowing every turn of the law. The lad was clever and articulate, but still very young. 'A child shouldn't go killing himself for the sake of religion.'

Both Berner and Grieve declined to cross-examine.

★ ★ ★

Before hearing closing submissions Fiona allowed a short break. The court rose and she went quickly to her room, drank a glass of water at her desk and checked her emails and texts. Plenty of both, but nothing from Jack. She searched again. It wasn't sadness or anger she felt now, but a dark hollowing out, an emptiness falling away behind her, threatening to annihilate her past.

Another phase. It didn't seem possible that the person she knew most intimately could be so cruel.

It was a relief, several minutes later, to be back in court. When Berner rose it was inevitable that he should move the argument to 'Gillick competence' — a point of reference in both family law and paediatrics. Lord Scarman had provided the formulation, and the barrister quoted him now. A child, that is, a person under sixteen, may consent to his or her own medical treatment 'if and when the child achieves sufficient understanding and intelligence to understand fully what is proposed'. If Berner, in advancing the hospital's case to treat Adam Henry against his wishes, was invoking Gillick now, it was to pre-empt Grieve doing so on behalf of the parents. Get in first and shape the terms. He did so in quick short sentences, his smooth tenor's voice as clear and precise as it was when he sang Goethe's tragic poem.

It was a given, Berner said, that not transfusing was of itself a form of treatment. None of the staff looking after Adam doubted his cleverness, his extraordinary way with words, his curiosity and passion for reading. He had won a poetry competition run by a serious national newspaper. He could recite a long part of an ode by Horace. He was truly an exceptional child. The court had heard the consultant confirm that here was an intelligent and articulate boy. Crucially, however, the doctor had just confirmed that Adam had only the vaguest notion of what would happen if he did not receive blood. He had a general, somewhat romantic, idea of the death that awaited him. Therefore he could not be said to fulfil the terms as set out by Lord Scarman. Adam most certainly did not 'understand fully what is proposed'. Quite rightly, the medical staff would not want to explain it to him. The senior health professional was in the best position to judge, and his conclusion was clear. Adam was not Gillick competent. Secondly, even if he was, and therefore had the right to assent to treatment, this was very different from the right to refuse life-saving treatment. On this the law was clear. He had no autonomy in the matter until he was eighteen.

Thirdly, it was plain, Berner continued, that the risks of infection following transfusion were minimal. Whereas the consequences of not transfusing were certain and horrific, probably fatal. And fourth, it was no coincidence that Adam happened to have the same particular faith as his parents. He was a loving and devoted son who had grown up in the atmosphere of their sincere and strongly held beliefs. His highly unconventional views concerning blood products, as the doctor had forcefully suggested, were not his own. All of us, surely, had beliefs at the age of seventeen that would embarrass us now.

Berner summarised at speed. Adam was not eighteen, did not understand the ordeal that lay ahead of him if he was not transfused, had been unduly influenced by the particular sect he had grown up in and was aware of the negative consequences should he defect. The views of Jehovah's Witnesses lay far outside those of a modern, reasonable parent.

As Mark Berner turned to sit down, Leslie Grieve was already on his feet. In his opening remarks, which he addressed a few feet to Fiona's left, he too wished to direct her attention to a pronouncement of Lord Scarman's. 'The existence of the patient's right to make his own decision may be seen as a basic human right, protected by the common law.' This court should therefore be extremely reluctant to interfere in a decision regarding medical treatment made by a person of evident intelligence and insight. It was plainly not enough to take shelter behind the two or three months that separated Adam from his eighteenth birthday. In a matter so gravely affecting an individual's basic human right, it was inappropriate to resort to number magic. This patient, who had repeatedly and consistently made his wishes clear, was far, far closer to being an eighteen-year-old than he was to being seventeen.

In an effort of memory, Grieve closed his eyes and quoted from Section 8 of the Family Reform Act of 1969. 'The consent of a minor who has attained the age of sixteen to any surgical, medical or dental treatment which, in the absence of consent, would constitute a trespass to his person, shall be effective as it would be if he were of full age.'

All those who met him, Grieve said, were struck by Adam's precocity and maturity. 'My Lady would be interested to know that he has read aloud some of his poems to the nursing staff. To great effect.' He was far more thoughtful than most seventeen-year-olds. It was necessary for the court to have regard to the position had he been born a few months earlier, when his fundamental right would have been secure. With the full support of his loving parents, he had made clear his objection to treatment and he had articulated in detail the religious principles on which his refusal rested.

Grieve paused, as if to reflect, then gestured towards the door through which the consultant had exited the courtroom. It was perfectly understandable for Mr Carter to despise the idea of withholding treatment. This merely demonstrated the professional devotion one would expect of so eminent a figure. But his professionalism clouded his judgement as to Adam's Gillick competence. Ultimately, this matter was not medical. It was legal and moral. It concerned a young man's inalienable right. He understood perfectly well where his decision could take him. To an early death. He had made himself clear many times. That he did not know the precise manner of his dying was beside the point. No one judged to be Gillick competent could be in full possession of that kind of knowledge. Indeed, nobody was. We all knew we would die one day. None of us knew how. And Mr Carter had already conceded that the team treating Adam would not wish to impart to him such an understanding. The young man's Gillick competence rested elsewhere, in his manifest grasp of the fact that refusing treatment could lead to his death. And Gillick, of course, rendered otiose the issue of his age.

So far, the judge had made three crowded pages of notes. One of these, on a separate line, was 'poetry?' Rising from the stream of argument was one bright image — supported by pillows, a teenage boy reading his verses to a tired nurse, who knew she was needed elsewhere but was too kind to say so.

Fiona had written poetry when she was Adam Henry's age, though she had never presumed to read it aloud, not even to herself. She remembered quatrains daringly unrhymed. There was even one about death by drowning, of sinking deliciously backwards among the river weeds, an improbable fantasy inspired by the Millais painting of Ophelia, before which she'd stood enraptured, during a school visit to the Tate. This daring poem in a crumbling notebook, on whose cover were doodles in purple ink of desirable hairstyles. As far as she knew, it lay at the bottom of a cardboard box, somewhere at the far end of the windowless spare room at home. If she could still call it home.

Grieve concluded that Adam was so near to eighteen as to make no difference. He satisfied the conditions articulated by Scarman, and was Gillick competent. The barrister quoted Balcombe LJ. 'As children approach the age of majority they are increasingly able to take their own decisions concerning their medical treatment. It will normally be in the best interests of a child of sufficient age and understanding to make an informed decision that the court should respect.' The court must take no view on a particular religion, save to respect expressions of faith. Nor should the court be tempted onto the dangerous ground of undermining an individual's basic right to refuse treatment.

Finally it was Tovey's turn and he was brief. With the help of his cane he pushed himself to a standing position. He represented both the boy and Marina Greene, the boy's guardian, and his tone was studiously neutral. The arguments for both sides had been well put by his colleagues and all relevant points in law had been covered. Adam's intelligence was not in question. His grasp of scripture as understood and propagated by his sect was thorough. It was important to consider that he was almost eighteen, but the fact remained, he was still a minor. It was therefore entirely for Her Ladyship to decide the weight she should apportion to the boy's wishes.

When the barrister sat down there was silence as Fiona glared at her notes, ordering her thoughts. Tovey had helpfully narrowed them to a decision. Addressing him, she said, 'Given the unique circumstances of this case, I've decided that I would like to hear from Adam Henry himself. It's not his knowledge of scripture that interests me so much as his understanding of his situation, and of what he confronts should I rule against the hospital. Also, he should know that he is not in the hands of an impersonal bureaucracy. I shall explain to him that I am the one who will be making the decision in his best interests.'

She went on to say that she would travel now with Mrs Greene to the hospital in Wandsworth and, in her presence, would sit at Adam Henry's bedside. Proceedings were therefore suspended until Fiona's return, when she would give judgment in open court.

3

This, Fiona decided as her taxi halted in heavy traffic on Waterloo Bridge, was either about a woman on the edge of a crack-up making a sentimental error of professional judgement, or it was about a boy delivered from or into the beliefs of his sect by the intimate intervention of the secular court. She didn't think it could be both. The question was suspended as she looked to her left, downstream towards St Paul's. The tide was running out fast. Wordsworth, on a nearby bridge, was right, either direction, best urban prospect in the world. Even in steady rain. At her side was Marina Greene. Beyond desultory small talk as they left the Courts of Justice, they had not spoken. Only proper, to keep a distance. And Greene, oblivious or well used to the upstream view on her right, was intent on her phone, reading, tapping, frowning in the contemporary manner.

On the South Bank side at last, they turned upriver at walking pace and took almost fifteen minutes to reach Lambeth Palace. Fiona's phone was off, which was her only defence against the compulsion to check texts and email every five minutes. She had written but not sent a message. *You cannot do this!* But he was doing it, and the exclamation mark said it all — she was a fool. Her emotional tone, as she sometimes referred to it and which she liked to monitor, was entirely novel. A blend of desolation and outrage. Or longing and fury. She wanted him back, she never wanted to see him again. Shame was also a component. But what had she done? Lost herself to work, neglected her husband, let one long case distract her? But he had his own work, he had his various moods. She had been humiliated and didn't want anyone to know and would pretend that all was fine. She felt tainted by secrecy. Was that it, was that the shame? Once in the know, one of her sensible friends was bound to urge her to phone him to demand an explanation. Impossible. She still recoiled from hearing the worst. Every thought she had now about the situation she'd indulged several times before, and still she went round again. Treadmill thinking, from which only sleep, medically induced, could rescue her. Sleep, or this unorthodox excursion.

At last they were on the Wandsworth Road and making twenty miles an hour, the speed of a horse at full gallop. They passed on the right an old cinema converted to squash courts where, many years ago, Jack had played to the limits of endurance to make eleventh place in an all-London tournament. And she, loyal young wife, somewhat bored, placed well back from the glass-fronted court, peeping from time to time at her notes on a rape case she was defending, and would lose. Eight years for her outraged client. Almost certainly blameless. Rightly, he never forgave her.

She had a north Londoner's ignorance of and disdain for the boundless shabby tangle of London south of the river. Not a Tube stop to give meaning and relation to a wilderness of villages swallowed up long ago, to sad shops, to dodgy garages interspersed with dusty Edwardian houses and brutalist apartment towers, the dedicated lairs of drug gangs. The pavement crowds, adrift in alien concerns, belonged to some other, remote city, not her own. How would she have known they were passing through Clapham Junction without the faded jokey sign above a boarded-up electrical store? Why make a life here? She recognised in herself the signs of an enveloping misanthropy and made herself remember her mission. She was visiting a seriously ill boy.

She liked hospitals. When she was thirteen, a keen high-speed cyclist to school, a slotted drain cover caused her to fly over her handlebars. A brief concussion and traces of blood in her urine kept her in hospital for observation. There was no room in the paediatric ward — a coachful of schoolchildren had returned from Spain with an unidentified stomach virus. She was put in with the women and remained among them for a week of undemanding tests. This was the mid 1960s, when the spirit of the times had not yet begun to question and unpick the starchy medical hierarchies. The high-ceilinged Victorian ward was clean and orderly, the frightening ward sister protective towards her youngest patient, and the old ladies, some of whom, it was clear in retrospect, were in their thirties, adored and cared for Fiona. She never considered their ailments. She was their pet and she was lost to a new existence. Her old routines of home and school dropped away. When one or two nice ladies vanished from their beds during the night she didn't think about it much. She was well protected from hysterectomies, cancer and death, and passed a glorious week without alarm or pain.

In the afternoons, after school, her friends would come, awed to be making a grown-up independent hospital visit. When the awe wore off, three or four girls would be round Fiona's bed shaking and clucking with held-down laughter at nothing much at all — a nurse striding by with a frown, the over-earnest greeting of an ancient lady with no teeth, someone at the far end of the ward being raucously sick behind a screen.

Before and after lunch, Fiona would sit alone in the day room with an exercise book on her lap, planning futures for herself — a concert pianist, a vet, a journalist, a singer. She made flow charts of possible lives. The trunk lines branched through university, heroic chunky husband, dreamy children, sheep farm, the eminent life. Back then she had not yet thought of the law.

On the day she was discharged, she went round the ward in school uniform, satchel swinging from her shoulder, watched by her mother, making tearful farewells and promises to stay in touch. In the decades that followed she was lucky in her health, and only ever in hospital during visiting hours. But she was marked for good. Whatever suffering and fear she saw in family and friends could not dislodge an improbable association of hospitals with kindness, with being noted as special, and sheltered from the worst. So now, inappropriately, as the twenty-six-storey Edith Cavell Wandsworth General rose above the misty oak trees on the far side of the common, she experienced a moment of pleasurable anticipation.

She and the social worker looked ahead, past the stuttering windscreen wipers, as the taxi approached a blue neon sign which announced remaining space for six hundred and fifteen cars. On a grassy rise, as on a Stone Age hill fort, stood the Japanese-designed circular tower of glass, with cladding of surgical-scrubs green, built with expensively borrowed money, back in the carefree days of New Labour. The highest floors were lost to the low-slung summer cloud.

As they walked towards the entrance a cat ran out in front of them from under a parked car and Marina Greene opened the conversation again to give a full account of her own cat, a bold British Shorthair that saw off all the dogs in the neighbourhood. Fiona warmed to this solemn young woman with the thin sandy hair who lived in a council house with her three children under five and her policeman husband. Her cat was beside the point. She was not letting anything prejudicial pass between them, but was sensitively aware of the shared concern they were about to confront.

Fiona allowed herself more freedom. She said, 'A cat that stands its ground. I hope you've told young Adam that story.'

Marina said quickly, 'I have, actually,' and fell silent.

They entered a glassed-in atrium the height of the entire building. Mature native trees, rather starved, pushed hopefully upwards from the concourse, from among the cheerful chairs and tables of competing coffee and sandwich concessions. Higher up, then even higher, other trees rose from concrete platforms cantilevered into the curving walls. The remotest plants were shrubs silhouetted against the glass roof three hundred feet up. The two women went across the pale parquet, past an information centre and an exhibition of unwell children's art. The long straight run of an escalator brought them to a mezzanine, where a bookshop, florist, newsagent, gift shop and business centre were ranged around a fountain. New Age music, airy and unmodulating, merged with the sound of tinkling water. The model was, of course, the modern airport. With altered destinations. At this level there was little sign of illness, none of medical equipment. The patients were finely spread between visitors and staff. Here and there were people in dressing gowns, looking rakish. Fiona and Marina followed signs with motorway lettering. *Paediatric Oncology, Nuclear Medicine, Phlebotomy.* They turned down a wide polished corridor that brought them to a bank of elevators and rode up in silence to the ninth floor, where an identical corridor took them through three left turns towards Intensive Care. They passed a jolly mural of apes swinging through a forest. Now, at last, the uncirculated air tasted of hospital, of cooked food long removed, antiseptic and, fainter, something sweet. Neither fruit nor flowers.

The nurses' station faced protectively onto a

semicircular array of closed doors, each one with an observation window. The silence, broken only by an electric hum, and the lack of natural light made it feel like the small hours. The two young nurses on the desk, one Filipina, Fiona later learned, the other Caribbean, exclaimed and greeted Marina with high fives. Suddenly the social worker was a different person, an animated black woman in a white skin. She spun round to introduce the judge to the young nurses as 'truly high up'. Fiona put out her hand. She could not have performed a high five without withering self-consciousness, and that seemed to be understood. Her hand was taken warmly. In a rapid exchange at the desk it was agreed that Fiona would remain outside while the social worker went in and explained things to Adam.

When Marina had gone through a door to the far right, Fiona turned to the nurses and asked about their young patient.

'He's learning the violin,' the young Filipina woman said. 'And driving us crazy!'

Her friend theatrically slapped her thigh. 'He's strangling a turkey in there.'

The nurses looked at each other and began to laugh, but quietly, out of consideration for their patients. This was clearly an old and coded joke. Fiona waited. She was feeling at home, but she knew it wouldn't last.

Finally she said, 'What about this transfusion business?'

All humour vanished. The Caribbean nurse said, 'I pray for him every day. I say to Adam, 'God don't need you to do this, darlin'. He loves

91

you anyway. God wants you to *live.*''

Her friend said sadly, 'He's made up his mind. You got to admire him. Living for his principles, is it.'

'Dying you mean! He knows nothing. This is one confused little puppy.'

Fiona said, 'What does he say when you tell him that God wants him to live?'

'Nothing. He's like, Why should I listen to *her?*'

Just then, Marina opened the door, raised a hand and went back inside.

Fiona said, 'Well, thank you.'

In response to a buzzer, the Filipina nurse was hurrying towards another door.

'You go in there, ma'm,' her friend said, 'and please turn him *around.* He's a lovely boy.'

If Fiona's recollection of stepping into Adam Henry's room was confused, it was because of the disorienting contrasts. There was much to take in. The place was in semi-darkness but for the focused bright light around the bed. In a corner, Marina was just settling herself into a chair with a magazine whose print she could not possibly read in such gloom. The life-support and monitoring equipment around the bed, the high stands, their feed lines and the glowing screens emanated a watchful presence, almost a silence. But there was no silence, for the boy was already talking to her as she entered, the moment was unfurling, or erupting, without her and she was left behind in a daze. He was sitting upright, supported by pillows against a metal backrest, lit as though by a single spot in a theatrical production. Spread about him on the sheets and spilling out into the shadows were books, pamphlets, a violin bow, a laptop, head-phones, orange peel, sweet wrappers, a box of tissues, a sock, a notebook and many lined pages covered in writing. Ordinary teenage squalor, familiar to her from family visits.

It was a long thin face, ghoulishly pale, but beautiful, with crescents of bruised purple fading delicately to white under the eyes, and full lips that appeared purplish too in the intense light. The eyes themselves looked violet and were huge. There was a mole high on one cheek, as artificial-looking as a painted beauty spot. His build was frail, his arms protruded like poles from the hospital gown. He spoke breathlessly, earnestly, and in those first few seconds she caught nothing. Then, as the door swung closed behind her with a pneumatic sigh, she gathered he was telling her how strange it was, he had known all along that she would visit him, that he thought he had this knack, this feel for the future, that they had read a poem at school in religious studies which said that the future, present and past were all one, and this was what the Bible said too. His chemistry teacher said relativity proved that time was an illusion. And if God, poetry and science all said the same thing, it had to be true, didn't she think?

He fell back against the pillows to catch his breath. She had been standing at the foot of his bed. Now she approached the side where there was a plastic chair and said her name and put out her hand. His was cold and damp. She sat down and waited for him to say more. But his head was tilted back and he was looking at the ceiling, still recovering and, she realised, expecting an answer. She became aware of the hiss of one of the machines at her back, as well as a muted rapid bleeping, at the audible threshold, or at least hers. The heart monitor, turned down for the patient's comfort, was betraying his excitement.

She leaned forward and said she thought he was right. In her experience in court, if different witnesses who had never spoken to each other all said the same thing about an event, it was more likely to be true.

Then she added, 'But it's not always. There can be group delusions. People who don't know each other can be gripped by the same false idea. That certainly happens in courts of law.'

'Like when?'

He was still catching his breath, and even these two words were an effort. His gaze remained upwards, away from her, while she thought of an example.

'Some years ago in this country children were taken away from their parents by the authorities, and the parents were prosecuted for what was called satanic abuse, for doing terrible things to their children in secret devil-worshipping rituals. Everyone piled in against the parents. Police, social workers, prosecutors, newspapers, even judges. But it turned out there was nothing. No secret rituals, no Satan, no abuse. Nothing had happened. It was a fantasy. All these experts and important people were sharing a delusion, a dream. Eventually, everyone came to their senses and was very ashamed, or they should have been. And very slowly, the children were returned to their homes.'

Fiona talked as though she herself was in a dream. She felt pleasantly tranquil, even as she guessed that Marina, monitoring the conversation, would be baffled by her remarks. What was the judge doing, talking to the boy about child abuse, within minutes of meeting him? Was she wanting to suggest that religion, his religion, was a group delusion? Marina would have expected the significant opening remark, after some gentle small talk, to be along the lines of, I'm sure you know why I'm here. Instead, Fiona was free-associating, as though to a colleague, about a forgotten institutional scandal of the 1980s. But what Marina thought did not really trouble her. She would do this her own way.

Adam lay still, taking in what she had said. At last, he turned his head on the pillow and his eyes met hers. She had squandered enough gravitas already and was determined not to look away. His breathing was more or less under control, his look was dark and solemn, impossible to read. That didn't matter, for she was feeling calmer than she had all day. No great claim. If not calm, then unhurried. The pressure of a waiting court, the necessity of a rapid decision, the consultant's urgent prognosis were temporarily suspended in the penumbral air-sealed room as she watched the boy and waited for him to speak. She was right to have come.

To hold his gaze for longer than half a minute

95

or so would have been improper, but she had time to imagine, in the condensing way of thought, what he saw in the chair by his bedside, another grown-up with a view, a grown-up further diminished by the special irrelevance that haunts an elderly lady.

He looked away just before saying, 'The thing about Satan is that he's amazingly sophisticated. He puts a stupid idea like satanic whatever, abuse, into people's minds, then he lets it get disproved so everyone thinks that he doesn't exist after all, and then he's free to do his worst.'

Another feature of her unorthodox opening — she had strayed onto his ground. Satan was a lively character in the Witness construction of the world. He had come down to earth, so she had read in her skim through the background material, in October 1914 in preparation for the end days and was working his evil through governments, the Catholic Church and especially the United Nations, encouraging it to sow concord among nations just when they should be readying themselves for Armageddon.

'He's free to try and kill you with leukaemia?'

She wondered if she had spoken too directly but he had an adolescent's affected resilience. Toughing it out. 'Yes. That sort of thing.'

'And you're going to let him?'

He pushed himself against the backrest to sit up, then stroked his chin thoughtfully, in parody of a pompous professor or TV pundit. He was mocking her.

'Well, since you ask, I intend to crush him by obeying God's commandments.'

'Is that a yes?'

He ignored this, waited a moment, then said, 'Have you come to change my mind, straighten me out?'

'Absolutely not.'

'Oh yes! I think so!' He was suddenly the mischievous provoking child, hugging his knees through the bedcovers, though feebly, and he was excited again, working up a sardonic voice. 'Please, Miss, set me on the path of righteousness.'

'I'll tell you why I'm here, Adam. I want to be sure you know what you're doing. Some people think you're too young to be taking a decision like this and that you've been influenced by your parents and the elders. And others think you're extremely clever and capable and we should just let you get on with it.'

In the harsh light he rose so vividly before her, the untidy black hair curling over the neckline of his gown, the large dark eyes scanning her face in restless saccades, alert for any deception or false notes. From the bedclothes she caught the scent of talcum powder or soap, and on his breath something thin and metallic. His diet of drugs.

'Well,' he said eagerly. 'What's your impression so far? How am I doing?'

He was playing her all right, drawing her back onto other ground, to a wilder space where he could dance round her, tempt her to say something inappropriate and interesting again. It occurred to her that this intellectually precocious young fellow was simply bored, under-stimulated, and that by threatening his own life he had set in motion a fascinating drama in which he starred in every scene, and which had brought to his bedside a parade of important and importuning adults. If this was so, she liked him all the more. Serious illness could not smother his vitality.

So, how was he doing? 'Pretty well, so far,' she said, aware she was taking a risk. 'You give the impression of someone who knows his own mind.'

'Thank you,' he said in a voice derisively sweet.

'But it might just be an impression.'

'I like to make a good impression.'

His manner, his humour, had an element of the silliness that can accompany high intelligence. And it was self-protective. He was surely very frightened. It was time to talk him down.

'And if you know your own mind, you won't object to discussing practicalities.'

'Fire away.'

'The consultant says that if he could transfuse you and raise your blood count he could add two very effective drugs to your treatment and you'd have a good chance of a complete and fairly quick recovery.'

'Yes.'

'And without a transfusion you could die. You understand that.'

'Yup.'

'And there's another possibility. I need to be sure you've considered it. Not death, Adam, but a partial recovery. You could lose your sight, you could suffer brain damage, or your kidneys could go. Would it please God, to have you blind or

98

stupid and on dialysis for the rest of your life?'

Her question overstepped the mark, the legal mark. She glanced across to where Marina sat in her shadowy corner. She was using the magazine to support a notebook and was writing by feel alone. She did not look up.

Adam was staring at a space over Fiona's head. With a wet clicking sound he moistened his lips with a white-coated tongue. Now there was sulkiness in his tone.

'If you don't believe in God you shouldn't be talking about what does or doesn't please him.'

'I haven't said I don't believe. I'd like to know whether you've considered this carefully, that you may be ill and disabled, mentally, physically or both, for the rest of your life.'

'I'd hate it, I'd hate it.' He turned from her quickly in the attempt to conceal the tears that had suddenly formed. 'But if that's what happens I have to accept it.'

He was upset, holding his gaze well away from her, ashamed that she could see how easy it had been to deflate his bumptiousness. His elbow, slightly crooked, looked pointed and fragile. Irrelevantly, she thought of recipes, roast chicken, with butter, tarragon and lemon, aubergines baked with tomatoes and garlic, potatoes lightly roasted in olive oil. Take this boy home and feed him up.

They had made useful progress, reached a new stage and she was about to follow up with another question when the Caribbean nurse came in and held the door wide open. Outside, as though summoned by her fantasy cuisine, was a young man in a brown cotton jacket, barely older than Adam, standing by a trolley of brushed steel containers.

'I can send your dinner away,' the nurse said. 'But only for half an hour.'

'If you can bear it,' Fiona said to Adam.

'I can bear it.'

She got up from her chair to allow the nurse to make her routine check on her patient and the monitors. She must have registered his emotional state and seen the wetness around his eyes, for she wiped his cheek with her hand just before she left and whispered loudly, 'You listen carefully to what this lady has to say.'

The interruption had altered the mood in the room. When Fiona was back in her chair she didn't return to her intended question. Instead she nodded towards the sheets of paper among the debris on the bed. 'I hear you've been writing poetry.'

She had expected him to reject the prompt as intrusive or condescending, but he seemed relieved to be diverted and she thought his manner was sincere, completely undefended. She also noted how quickly his mood shifted.

'I've just finished something. I could read it if you want. It's really short. But wait a minute.' He rolled onto his side to face her directly. Before speaking he wetted his dried lips. Again, the creamy white tongue. In another context it might have been beautiful, a cosmetic novelty.

He said confidingly, 'What do they call you in court? Is it 'Your Honour'?'

'Usually it's 'My Lady'.'

'My Lady? That's fantastic! Am I allowed to call you that?'

'Fiona will do.'

'But I want to call you My Lady. Please let me.'

'All right. What about this poem?'

He leaned back against the pillows to get his breath back and she waited. Reaching forwards at last for a sheet of paper near his knee brought on a round of enfeebled coughing. When that was done his voice was thin and husky. She heard no irony in the way he now addressed her.

'The weird thing, My Lady, is that I didn't start writing my best poetry until I got ill. Why do you think that is?'

'You tell me.'

He shrugged. 'I like writing in the middle of the night. The whole building shuts down and all you can hear is this strange deep hum. You can't hear it in the day. Listen.'

They listened. Outside, there were still another four hours of light and rush hour was peaking. In here it was the dead of night, but she could hear no hum. She was coming to realise that his defining quality was innocence, a fresh and excitable innocence, a childlike openness that may have had something to do with the enclosed nature of the sect. The congregation, so she had read, was encouraged to keep their children apart as far as was possible from outsiders. Rather like the ultra-Orthodox Jews. Her own teenage relatives, girls as well as boys, had all too soon protected themselves with a sheen of knowing toughness. Their overstated cool was charming in its way, a necessary bridge to adulthood. Adam's unworldliness made him endearing, but vulnerable. She was touched by his delicacy, by the way he stared fiercely at his sheet of paper, perhaps trying to hear in advance his poem through her ears. She decided that he was probably much loved at home.

He glanced at her, drew breath and began.

My fortunes sank into the darkest hole
When Satan took his hammer to my soul.
His blacksmith's strokes were long and slow
And I was low.

But Satan made a cloth of beaten gold
That shone God's love upon the fold.
The way with golden light is paved
And I am saved.

She waited in case there was more but he put the page down, leaned back and looked at the ceiling as he spoke.

'I wrote it after one of the elders, Mr Crosby, told me that if the worst was to happen, it would have a fantastic effect on everyone.'

Fiona murmured, 'He said that?'

'It would fill our church with love.'

She summed up for him. 'So Satan comes to beat you with his hammer, and without meaning to he flattens your soul into a sheet of gold that reflects God's love on everyone and for this you're saved and it doesn't matter so much that you're dead.'

'My Lady, you've got it exactly,' the boy almost shouted in his excitement. Then he had to stop to recover his breath again. 'I don't think the nurses understood it, except for Donna, the one who was in here just now. Mr Crosby's going to try and get it published in *The Watchtower*.'

'That would be marvellous. You may have a future as a poet.'

He saw through this and smiled.

'What do your parents think of your poems?'

'My mum loves them, my dad thinks they're okay but they use up the strength I need to get better.' He rolled onto his side again to face her. 'But what does My Lady think? It's called 'The Hammer'.'

He had such a hunger in his look, such longing for her approval that she hesitated. Then she said, 'I think it shows a touch, a very small touch, mind, of real poetic genius.'

He continued to gaze at her, expression unchanged, wanting more. She had thought she knew what she was doing, but just then her mind emptied. She didn't want to disappoint him and she was not used to talking about poetry.

He said, 'What makes you say that?'

She didn't know, not immediately. She would have appreciated Donna returning to bustle around the machines and her patient, while she herself went to the unopenable window and looked out across Wandsworth Common and decided what to say. But the nurse was not due for another fifteen minutes. Fiona hoped that by starting to speak she would discover what she thought. It was like being at school. Back then she had mostly got away with it.

'The shape, the form of it, and those two short lines balancing things out, you're low then you're saved, the second overcoming the first, I liked that. And I liked the blacksmith's strokes . . . '

'Long and slow.'

'Mm. Long and slow is good. And it's very condensed, the way some of the best short poems are.' She felt some confidence returning. 'I suppose it's telling us that out of adversity, out of a terrible time, something good can come. Isn't that right?'

'Yes.'

'And I don't think you have to believe in God to understand or like this poem.'

He thought for a moment and said, 'I think you do.'

She said, 'Do you think you have to suffer to be a good poet?'

'I think all great poets must suffer.'

'I see.'

By pretending to adjust her sleeve she exposed her wristwatch and glanced down at it on her lap without seeming to. She must soon return to the waiting court and give her judgment.

But he had seen her. 'Don't go yet,' he said in a whisper. 'Wait till my supper comes.'

'All right. Adam, tell me, what do your parents think?'

'My mum is better at dealing with it. She accepts things, you know? Submission to God. And she's very practical, making all the arrangements, talking to the doctors, getting me this room, larger than the others, finding me a violin. But my dad is sort of tearing himself apart. He's used to being in charge of earth movers and stuff and making things work.'

'And refusing a transfusion?'

104

'What about it?'

'What do your parents say to you?'

'There isn't much to say. We know what's right.'

As he said this, looking at her directly, with no particular challenge in his voice, she believed him completely, he and his parents, the congregation and the elders knew what was right for them. She felt unpleasantly light-headed, emptied out, all meaning gone. The blasphemous notion came to her that it didn't much matter either way whether the boy lived or died. Everything would be much the same. Profound sorrow, bitter regret perhaps, fond memories, then life would plunge on and all three would mean less and less as those who loved him aged and died, until they meant nothing at all. Religions, moral systems, her own included, were like peaks in a dense mountain range seen from a great distance, none obviously higher, more important, truer than another. What was to judge?

She shook her head to dispel the thought. Waiting in reserve was the question she had been about to ask before Donna came in. As soon as she started to pose it, she felt better.

'Your father explained some of the religious arguments, but I want to hear it in your own words. Why exactly won't you have a blood transfusion?'

'Because it's wrong.'

'Go on.'

'And God has told us it's wrong.'

'Why is it wrong?'

'Why is anything wrong? Because we know it.

Torture, murder, lying, stealing. Even if we get good information out of bad people by torturing them, we know it's wrong. We know it because God has instructed us. Even if — '

'Is transfusion the same as torture?'

Marina stirred in her corner. Adam, speaking in breathy snatches, set out on his exposition. Transfusion and torture were only similar in that they were both wrong. We knew it in our hearts. He quoted Leviticus and Acts, he talked about blood as the essence, about the literal word of God, about pollution, he held forth like a clever sixth-former, the star pupil in the school debate. His violet black eyes shone as his own words moved him. Fiona recognised certain phrases from the father. But Adam spoke them like the discoverer of elementary facts, the formulator of doctrine rather than its recipient. It was a sermon she was hearing, faithfully and passionately reproduced. He presented himself as a spokesman for his sect when he said that he and his congregation just wanted to be left alone to live by what they knew to be self-evident truths.

Fiona was attentive, she held the boy's gaze, nodded occasionally, and when at last there was a natural pause, she stood and said, 'Just to be clear, Adam. You do realise that it's for me alone to decide what's in your best interests. If I were to rule that the hospital may legally transfuse you against your wishes, what will you think?'

He was sitting up, breathing hard and seemed to sag a little at the question, but he smiled. 'I'd think My Lady was an interfering busybody.'

It was such an unexpected change of register,

so absurdly understated, and her own surprise so obvious to him, that they both began to laugh. Marina, just then gathering up her handbag and notebook, seemed puzzled.

Fiona looked at her watch, openly this time. She said, 'I think you've made it pretty clear that you know your own mind, as much as any of us ever can.'

He said with proper solemnity, 'Thank you. I'll tell my parents tonight. But don't go. My supper isn't here yet. What about another poem?'

'Adam, I have to get back to court.' But she was keen all the same to turn the conversation away from his condition. She saw the bow lying on his bed, partly in shadow.

'Quickly, before I go, show me your violin.'

The case was on the floor by a locker, under the bed. She lifted it up and placed it on his lap.

'It's only a school violin for beginners.' But he brought it out with extreme care and showed it to her and together they admired the contoured nut-brown wood edged with black and the delicate scrolls.

She laid her hand on the lacquered surface and he put his close to hers. She said, 'They're beautiful instruments. I always think there's something so human about the shape.'

He was reaching for his beginners' violin tutor from the locker. She hadn't intended for him to play, but she couldn't stop him. His illness, his innocent eagerness made him impregnable.

'I've been learning for four weeks exactly and I can play ten tunes.' His boast too made it impossible to deflect him. He was turning the pages impatiently. Fiona looked over at Marina and shrugged.

'But this one is the hardest yet. Two sharps. D major.'

Fiona was looking at the music upside down. She said, 'It might just be B minor.'

He didn't hear her. He was already sitting up, with the violin tucked under his chin, and without pausing to tune the strings, he began to play. She knew it well, this sad and lovely melody, a traditional Irish air. She had accompanied Mark Berner in Benjamin Britten's setting of the Yeats poem 'Down by the Salley Gardens'. It was one of their encores. Adam played it scratchily, without vibrato, of course, but the pitch of the notes was true even though two or three were wrong. The melancholy tune and the manner in which it was played, so hopeful, so raw, expressed everything she was beginning to understand about the boy. She knew by heart the poet's words of regret. *But I, being young and foolish* . . . Hearing Adam play stirred her, even as it baffled her. To take up the violin or any instrument was an act of hope, it implied a future.

When he finished she and Marina applauded and from his bed Adam made an awkward bow.

'Stupendous!'

'Fantastic!'

'And only four weeks!'

Fiona, in order to contain the emotion she felt, added a technical point. 'Remember that in this key the C is sharp.'

'Oh yes. So many things to think of at once.'

Then she made a proposal that was far removed from anything she would have expected of herself, and which risked undermining her authority. The situation, and the room itself, sealed off from the world, in perpetual dusk, may have encouraged a mood of abandon, but above all, it was Adam's performance, his look of straining dedication, the scratchy inexpert sounds he made, so expressive of guileless longing, that moved her profoundly and prompted her impulsive suggestion.

'So play it again, and this time I'll sing along with you.'

Marina got to her feet, frowning, perhaps wondering whether she should intervene.

Adam said, 'I didn't know there were words.'

'Oh yes, two beautiful verses.'

With touching solemnity, he raised the violin to his chin and looked up at her. When he began to play she was pleased to hear herself find the higher notes easily. She had always been secretly proud of her voice, and never had much chance to use it outside the Gray's Inn choir, back when she was still a member. This time the violinist remembered his C sharp. On the first verse they were tentative, almost apologetic, but on the second, their eyes met and, forgetting all about Marina, who was now standing by the door, looking on amazed, Fiona sang louder and Adam's clumsy bowing grew bolder, and they swelled into the mournful spirit of the backward-looking lament.

In a field by the river my love and I did stand,
And on my leaning shoulder she laid her

snow-white hand.
She bid me take life easy, as the grass grows on the weirs;
But I was young and foolish, and now am full of tears.

As they finished, the lad in the brown jacket was rolling his trolley into the room and the brushed-steel plate-covers made a cheerful tinkling sound. Marina had gone out to the nurses' station.

Adam said, '"On my leaning shoulder" is good, isn't it? Let's do it again.'

Fiona shook her head as she took the violin from him and laid it in its case. '"She bid me take life easy",' she quoted to him.

'Stay just a tiny bit longer. Please.'

'Adam, I really do have to go now.'

'Then let me have your email.'

'Mrs Justice Maye, Royal Courts of Justice, the Strand. That'll find me.'

She rested her hand briefly on his narrow cold wrist, then, not wanting to hear another protest or plea from him, she went towards the door without looking back, and ignored the question he called weakly after her.

'Are you coming back?'

★ ★ ★

The return journey to central London was quicker and during it the two women did not speak. While Marina made a long phone call to her husband and children, Fiona wrote notes towards her judgment. She entered the Courts of Justice

110

by the main entrance and went immediately to her room, where Nigel Pauling was waiting. He confirmed that all the arrangements were in place for the Court of Appeal to sit tomorrow, if necessary at an hour's notice. Also, tonight the hearing had been moved to a court large enough to accommodate all the press.

When she entered and the court rose it was just after nine fifteen. As the room settled she sensed impatience among the journalists. For the newspapers, this was not a convenient time. At best, if the judge was succinct, the story might make the late editions. Immediately in front of her, the various legal representation and Marina Greene were arranged as before, within a wider space, but Mr Henry was alone behind his counsel, without his wife.

As soon as she sat, Fiona began her routine introductory remarks.

'A hospital authority urgently requires the permission of the court to treat against his wishes a teenage boy, A, with conventional procedures they deem medically appropriate, which in this case includes blood transfusions. They're looking for this relief under a Specific Issue Order. The application, made forty-eight hours ago, was on an *ex parte* basis. As duty judge, I granted it, subject to their undertakings. I have just returned from visiting A in hospital, accompanied by Mrs Marina Greene for Cafcass. I sat with him for an hour. That he's extremely ill is plain to see. However, his intellect is in no way impaired and he was able to make his wishes known to me with great clarity. The

111

treating consultant has told this court that by tomorrow A's situation will have become a matter of life and death, which is why I give judgment so late on a Tuesday evening.'

Fiona named and thanked the various counsel, their solicitors, Marina Greene and the hospital for helping her come to a decision in a difficult case that had to be speedily resolved.

'The parents oppose the application on the basis of their religious faith, which is calmly expressed and profoundly held. Their son also objects and has a good understanding of the religious principles and is possessed of considerable maturity and articulacy for his age.'

She then set out the medical history, the leukaemia, the recognised treatment for which generally had good outcomes. But two of the drugs conventionally administered caused anaemia, which needed to be countered by blood transfusion. She summarised the consultant's evidence, noting in particular the declining haemoglobin count and the dire prognosis if it was not reversed. She could personally confirm that A's breathlessness was now apparent.

The opposition to the application rested on three principal arguments. That A was three months short of his eighteenth birthday, was highly intelligent, understood the consequences of his decision and should be treated as being Gillick competent. In other words, as worthy of recognition for his decisions as any adult. That refusing medical treatment was a fundamental human right and a court should therefore be reluctant to intervene. And thirdly, that A's religious faith was genuine and should be respected.

Fiona addressed these in turn. She thanked counsel for A's parents for bringing to her attention the relevant Section 8 of the Family Reform Act of 1969: the consent of a sixteen-year-old to treatment 'shall be as effective as it would be if he were of full age'. She set out the conditions of Gillick competence, quoting Scarman along the way. She recognised a distinction between a competent child under sixteen consenting to treatment, possibly against the wishes of its parents, and a child under eighteen refusing life-saving treatment. From what she had gathered that evening, did she find A to have a complete grasp of the implications of having his and his parents' wishes granted?

'He is without doubt an exceptional child. I might even say, as one of the nurses did this evening, that he is a lovely boy, and I'm sure his parents would agree. He possesses exceptional insight for a seventeen-year-old. But I find that he has little concept of the ordeal that would face him, of the fear that would overwhelm him as his suffering and helplessness increased. In fact, he has a romantic notion of what it is to suffer. However . . . '

She let the word hang, and the silence in the room tightened as she glanced down at her notes.

'However, I am not ultimately influenced by whether he has or doesn't have a full comprehension of his situation. I am guided instead by the decision of Mr Justice Ward, as he then was, in Re E (a minor), a judgment also concerning a

Jehovah's Witness teenager. In the course of which he notes, 'The welfare of the child therefore dominates my decision, and I must decide what E's welfare dictates.' That observation was crystallised in the clear injunction of the Children Act of 1989 which declares in its opening lines for the primacy of the child's welfare. I take 'welfare' to encompass 'well-being' and 'interests'. I'm also bound to take into account A's wishes. As I've already noted, he has expressed them clearly to me, as has his father to this court. In accordance with the doctrines of his religion derived from a particular interpretation of three passages in the Bible, A refuses the blood transfusion that will likely save his life.

'It is a fundamental right in adults to refuse medical treatment. To treat an adult against his will is to commit the criminal offence of assault. A is close to the age when he may make the decision for himself. That he is prepared to die for his religious beliefs demonstrates how deep they are. That his parents are prepared to sacrifice a dearly loved child for their faith reveals the power of the creed to which Jehovah's Witnesses adhere.'

Again she stopped and the public gallery waited.

'It is precisely this power that gives me pause, for A, at seventeen, has sampled little else in the turbulent realm of religious and philosophical ideas. It is not part of the methods of this Christian sect to encourage open debate and dissent among the congregation at large, which is referred to by them, aptly some might say, as 'the

114

other sheep'. I do not believe that A's mind, his opinions, are entirely his own. His childhood has been an uninterrupted monochrome exposure to a forceful view of the world and he cannot fail to have been conditioned by it. It will not promote his welfare to suffer an agonising unnecessary death, and so become a martyr to his faith. The Jehovah's Witnesses, like other religions, have a clear notion of what awaits us after death, and their predictions of the end days, their eschatology, are also firm and very detailed. This court takes no view on the afterlife, which in any event A will discover, or fail to discover, for himself one day. Meanwhile, assuming a good recovery, his welfare is better served by his love of poetry, by his newly found passion for the violin, by the exercise of his lively intelligence and the expressions of a playful, affectionate nature, and by all of life and love that lie ahead of him. In short, I find that A, his parents and the elders of the church have made a decision which is hostile to A's welfare, which is this court's paramount consideration. He must be protected from such a decision. He must be protected from his religion and from himself.

'This has been no easy matter to resolve. I have given due weight to A's age, to the respect due to faith, and to the dignity of the individual embedded in the right to refuse treatment. In my judgement, his life is more precious than his dignity.

'Consequently, I overrule the wishes of A and his parents. My direction and declaration are as follows: that the agreement to blood transfusion of the first and second respondents, who are the parents, and the agreement to blood transfusion of the third respondent, who is A himself, are set aside. Therefore it will be lawful for the applicant hospital to pursue the medical treatments of A they regard necessary, on the understanding that these may entail the administration of blood and its products by transfusion.'

★　★　★

It was almost eleven o'clock when Fiona set off to walk home from the Courts of Justice. At this hour, the gates were locked and it wasn't possible to cut through Lincoln's Inn. Before turning up Chancery Lane she went a short way along Fleet Street to an all-night convenience store to buy a ready-made meal. The night before, it would have been a bleak mission, but she was feeling almost carefree, perhaps because she hadn't eaten properly in two days. In the cramped, over-lit shop, the garish packaged goods, the explosive reds and purples and starburst yellows throbbed on the shelves to the beat of her pulse. She bought a frozen fish pie and weighed up various fruits in her hand before deciding. At the checkout she fumbled with her money, spilling coins onto the floor. The nimble Asian lad working at the till trapped them neatly with his foot, and smiled protectively at her as he put the money in her palm. She imagined herself through his eyes as he took in her exhausted look, ignoring or unable to read the tailored cut of her jacket, seeing clearly one of those harmless biddies who lived and ate alone, no longer quite capable, out in the world far too late at night.

She was humming 'The Salley Gardens' as she went along High Holborn. The fruit and the dense hard package of her supper swinging in its carrier bag against her leg was a comfort. The pie could cook in the microwave while she prepared for bed, she would eat in her dressing gown in front of a rolling-news channel, and then nothing would stand between her and sleep. No chemical prompt. Tomorrow was a high-end divorce, a famous guitarist, an almost famous wife, a torch singer with an excellent solicitor, wanting some large portion of his twenty-seven million. Candy-floss compared to today, but the press interest would be just as intense, the law just as solemn.

She turned into Gray's Inn, her familiar sanctuary. It always pleased her, the way the city's traffic rumble died away as she went deeper in. A gated community of a historical sort, a fortress of barristers and judges who were also musicians, wine-fanciers, would-be writers, fly fishermen and raconteurs. A nest of gossip and expertise, and a delightful garden still haunted by the reasonable spirit of Francis Bacon. She loved it here and never wanted to leave.

She entered her building, noted that the time switch for the lights was on, walked up towards the second floor, heard the usual jagged creak on the fourth and seventh stairs, and on the final run to her landing saw everything and immediately understood. Her husband was there, just getting to his feet, a book in his hand, and behind him against the wall, his suitcase had been a kind

117

of seat, and his jacket was on the floor beside his briefcase, which was open, with papers spilling out. Locked out, working while waiting. And why not? He looked rumpled and irritated. Locked out and waiting a very long time. Clearly not back for fresh shirts and books, not with his suitcase there. Her immediate thought, a gloomy and selfish one, was that now she would have to share her single-portion supper. And then she thought she wouldn't. She'd rather not eat.

She came up the last few stairs onto the landing, saying nothing as she reached for her keys, the new keys, from her bag, stepped around him and went to the door. It was for him to speak first.

His tone was querulous. 'I've been phoning you all evening.'

She unlocked the door and walked in without looking back and went into the kitchen, dumped her stuff on the table and paused there. Her heart was beating far too hard. She heard his bad-tempered breathing as he brought in his luggage. If there was to be a confrontation, which she didn't want, not now, the kitchen was too confined a space. She took her briefcase and went quickly into the sitting room, to her usual place on the chaise longue. Spreading a few papers around where she sat was a form of protection. Without them she would not know what to do with herself.

The rumble of Jack towing his suitcase further along the hall and into their bedroom seemed to her like an opening move. And an insult. By force of habit, she pulled off her shoes, then took up a document at random. The guitarist had a pleasantly appointed villa in Marbella. The torch singer rather fancied it for herself. But he had acquired it before the marriage, from his previous wife in return for vacating the family home in central London. And that previous wife had come by it in a divorce settlement with her first husband. Irrelevant, Fiona couldn't help herself ruling.

At a creak of a floorboard she glanced up. Jack paused in the doorway before heading for the drinks. He wore jeans and a white shirt unbuttoned to his chest. Did he imagine he was desirable? She noticed he hadn't shaved. Even from across the room, his bristles showed white and grey. Pathetic, they were both pathetic. He poured himself a Scotch and raised the bottle in her direction. She shook her head. He shrugged and crossed the room to his chair. She was a spoilsport, no sense of occasion. He sat down with a homely sigh. His chair, her chair, married life again. She looked at the paper in her hand, the wife's narrative of the guitarist's desirable world, impossible to take in. There was silence while he drank and she stared across the room at nothing in particular.

Then he said, 'Look, Fiona, I love you.'

After several seconds she said, 'I'd rather you slept in the spare room.'

He lowered his head in assent. 'I'll move my case.'

He did not get up. They both knew the vitality of the unsaid, whose invisible spirits danced around them now. She had not told him to keep

119

out of the flat, she had tacitly agreed he could sleep there. He had not told her yet whether his statistician had thrown him out or he had changed his mind or indulged sufficient ecstatic experience to see him to his grave. The change of locks had not been touched on. He was probably suspicious of her being out so late. She could barely stand the sight of him. What was required now was a row, one with several chapters stretching over time. There might be some rancorous digressions, his contrition might come wrapped in complaints, it might be months before she would allow him in her bed, the ghost of the other woman might linger between them for ever. But they would likely find a way of being back, more or less, with what they once had.

Contemplating the mighty effort involved, the predictability of the process, wearied her further. And yet she was bound to it. As to a contract she must fulfil to write a boring, necessary legal manual. She thought she would like a drink after all, but that might have looked too much like a celebration. She was a long way from being reconciled. Above all, she could not bear to hear again that he loved her. She wanted to be in bed alone, on her back in the dark, biting into some fruit, letting the remains drop to the floor, then passing out. What was to stop her? She stood and began to gather up her papers, and it was then that he began to speak.

It was a torrent, part apology, part self-justification, some of which she had heard before. His mortality, his years of complete fidelity, his overwhelming curiosity about how it would be, and almost as soon as he left that night, as soon as he arrived at Melanie's place, he realised his mistake. She was a stranger, he didn't understand her. And when they went into her bedroom . . .

Fiona raised a warning hand. She didn't want to hear about the bedroom. He paused, considered, and continued. He was a fool, he realised, to be driven by sexual need and he should have turned on his heel that night, when she opened her door to him, but he was embarrassed and felt bound to continue.

Clutching her briefcase against her stomach, Fiona stood in the centre of the room, watching him, wondering how to stop him. It amazed her that even now, with the high marital drama in its opening scene, the Irish song continued to turn in her mind, quickening to the rhythm of Jack's speech, and sounding both mechanical and festive, as though cranked out by a street organ grinder. Her feelings were in confusion, blurred by fatigue and hard to define as long as her husband's plaintive words swept over her. She felt something less than fury or bitter resentment, and yet it was more than mere resignation.

Yes, Jack said, once he arrived at Melanie's flat he felt stupidly obliged to go on with what he had started. 'And the more trapped I felt, the more I realised what an idiot I was to risk everything we have, everything we've made together, this love that — '

'I've had a long day,' she said as she crossed the room. 'I'll put your suitcase in the hall.'

She stopped by the kitchen to take an apple

and a banana from her shopping on the table. Having them in her hand as she went towards the bedroom brought back her relatively happy walk home from work. She had felt the beginnings of some ease. Hard to recapture now. She pushed open the door and saw his suitcase standing upright and prim on its wheels by the bed. Then it came to her plainly what she felt about Jack's return. So simple. It was disappointment that he had not stayed away. Just a little longer. Nothing more than that. Disappointment.

4

It was her impression, though the facts did not bear it out, that in the late summer of 2012, marital or partner breakdown and distress in Great Britain swelled like a freak spring tide, sweeping away entire households, scattering possessions and hopeful dreams, drowning those without a powerful instinct for survival. Loving promises were denied or rewritten, once easy companions became artful combatants crouching behind counsel, oblivious to the costs. Once neglected domestic items were bitterly fought for, once easy trust was replaced by carefully worded 'arrangements'. In the minds of the principals, the history of the marriage was redrafted to have been always doomed, love was recast as delusion. And the children? Counters in a game, bargaining chips for use by mothers, objects of financial or emotional neglect by fathers; the pretext for real or fantasised or cynically invented charges of abuse, usually by mothers, sometimes by fathers; dazed children shuttling weekly between households in co-parenting agreements, mislaid coats or pencil cases shrilly broadcast by one solicitor to another; children doomed to see their fathers once or twice a month; or never, as the most purposeful men vanished into the smithy of a hot new marriage to forge new offspring.

And the money? The new coinage was half-truth and special pleading. Greedy husbands versus greedy wives, manoeuvring like nations at the end of a war, grabbing from the ruins what spoils they could before the final withdrawal. Men concealing their funds in foreign accounts, women demanding a life of ease, for ever. Mothers preventing children from seeing their fathers, despite court orders; fathers neglecting to support their children, despite court orders. Husbands hitting wives and children, wives lying and spiteful, one party or the other or both drunk, or drug-addled, or psychotic; and children again, forced to become carers of an inadequate parent, children genuinely abused, sexually, mentally, both, their evidence relayed on screen to the court. And beyond Fiona's reach, in cases reserved for the criminal rather than the family courts, children tortured, starved or beaten to death, evil spirits thrashed out of them in animist rites, gruesome young stepfathers breaking toddlers' bones while dim compliant mothers looked on, and drugs, drink, extreme household squalor, indifferent neighbours selectively deaf to the screaming, and careless or hard-pressed social workers failing to intervene.

The work of the Family Division went on. It was an accident of the listings that so much marital conflict came Fiona's way. Pure coincidence that she was in conflict herself. It was not usual in this line of work to be sending people to prison, but all the same, she thought in idle moments that she could send down all those parties wanting, at the expense of their children, a younger wife, a richer or less boring husband, a different suburb, fresh sex, fresh love, a new world view, a nice new start before it was too late. Mere pursuit of pleasure. Moral kitsch. Her own childlessness and the situation with Jack shaped these daydreams and, of course, she was not serious. Still, she buried deep in a private mental domain, but never let it affect her decisions, a puritan contempt for the men and women who pulled their families apart and persuaded themselves they were acting selflessly for the best. In this thought experiment, she wouldn't have spared the childless, or at least, not Jack. A cleansing spell in the Scrubs for contaminating their marriage in the cause of novelty? Why not?

For life at home in Gray's Inn since his return was quiet and strained. There had been rows, during which she discharged some bitter feelings. Twelve hours later those feelings were renewed as ardently as wedding vows, and nothing changed, the air was not 'cleared'. She remained betrayed. He spiced his apologies with old complaints that she had isolated him, that she was cold. He even said late one night that she was 'no fun' and had 'lost the art of play'. Of all his accusations, these bothered her most because she sensed their truth, but they did not diminish her anger.

At least he was no longer saying he loved her. Their most recent exchange, ten days ago, reiterated all they had said before, every charge, every response, every brooded-over well-turned phrase, and in a short while they fell back, weary with each other and themselves. Since then, nothing. They moved about their days, their separate business in different parts of the city, and when confined together in the apartment, stepped daintily around each other, like dancers at a hoedown. They were terse and competitively polite when obliged to confer on household matters, avoided meals together, worked in separate rooms, each distracted by raw awareness through the walls of the other's radioactive presence. Without discussing it, they ducked out of all joint invitations. Her only conciliatory move was to give him a new key.

She inferred from his evasive but morose remarks that in the statistician's bedroom he had not passed through the gates of paradise. Not really so reassuring. He was likely to try his luck elsewhere, was trying it already perhaps, freed this time from the dismal constraints of honesty. His 'geology lectures' may have been a useful cover. She remembered her promise to leave him if he went ahead with Melanie. But Fiona didn't have the time to set in motion such a gross disentanglement. And she was still undecided, she didn't trust her current mood. If he had given her more time after he left, she would have reached a clear decision and worked constructively to end the marriage or rebuild it. So she abandoned herself to work in the usual way and set herself to survive a day at a time the subdued drama of her half-life with Jack.

When one of his nieces dropped off her children for the weekend, identical twin girls aged eight, matters became easier, the apartment grew larger as attention turned outwards. For two nights Jack slept on the sofa in the sitting room, which the children never questioned.

126

These were girls of a straight-backed old-fashioned sort, solemn and intimate in their manner, though not above the occasional explosive row. One or the other — they were easy to tell apart — would seek Fiona out where she was reading, and stand before her, resting a confiding hand on her knee, and release a silvery stream of anecdote, reflection, fantasy. Fiona would join in with stories of her own. Twice on this visit it happened that while she was speaking, a wave of love for the child constricted her throat and pricked her eyes. She was feeling old and foolish. It bothered her to be reminded how good Jack was with children. At the risk of putting his back out, the way he did once with Fiona's brother's three boys, he indulged some wild horseplay, which the girls took to with fits of inhuman shrieking. At home, their resentfully divorced mother never tossed them in the air upside down. He took them into the gardens to teach them an eccentric version of cricket he'd devised, and he read a long bedtime tale with booming comic energy and a talent for the voices.

But on Sunday evening, after the twins had been picked up, the rooms shrank back, the air was stale and Jack went out without explanation — surely a hostile act. To an assignation, she wondered as she made herself busy, tidying the spare room to keep her spirits from lowering further. Restoring the soft toys to the wicker basket where they lived, retrieving glass beads and discarded drawings from under the bed, she felt the mild enveloping sorrow, a form of instant nostalgia, that the sudden absence of children can bring on. That feeling lingered into Monday morning and swelled into a general sadness that followed her on the walk to work. It only began to fade when she sat at her desk to prepare for her first case of the week.

At some point, Nigel Pauling must have brought in the post, for the pile was suddenly there at her elbow. At the sight of an undersized pale blue envelope resting on top, she almost called her clerk back to open it. She was in no mood to read for herself one more outpouring of illiterate abuse or a threat of violence. She turned back to her work, but couldn't concentrate. The impractical envelope, loopy hand, absent post-code, the postage stamp slightly awry — she'd seen too much of it. But when she looked again and noticed the postmark she had a sudden suspicion, weighed the letter in her hand a moment, and opened it. Instantly, she saw from the salutation that she was right. She had vaguely expected it for weeks. She'd spoken to Marina Greene and learned that he was making good progress, out of hospital, catching up on schoolwork at home, and expected back in his classroom within weeks.

Three pale blue pages, with writing on five sides. The first had a circled number seven centred at the top, above the date.

My Lady!
This is my seventh and I think it's going to be the one that I post.

The first several words of the next paragraph were scored out.

It will be the simplest and the shortest. I only want to describe to you one event. I realise now how important it is. It's changed everything. I'm glad I waited because I wouldn't like you to see the other letters. Too embarrassing! But not as terrible as all the names I called you when Donna came and told me your decision. I was sure you'd seen things my way. In fact I know exactly what you told me, that it was obvious that I knew my own mind and I remember thanking you. I was still raging and ranting when that awful consultant, Mister 'call-me-Rodney' Carter, came in with half a dozen others and the equipment. They thought they were going to have to hold me down. But I was too feeble for that, and even though I was furious, I knew what you wanted me to do. So I held out my arm and they got started. The thought of someone else's blood going into mine was so disgusting that I was sick right across the bed.

But that isn't the one thing I wanted to tell you. It's this. My mum couldn't bear to watch so she was sitting outside my room and I could hear her crying and I felt really sad. I don't know when my dad turned up. I think I passed out for a while and when I came round they were both there by my bed — and they were both crying and I felt even sadder, for all of us for disobeying God. But this is the important thing, it took me a moment to realise that they were crying for

JOY! They were so so happy, hugging me, and hugging each other and praising God and sobbing. I was feeling too weird and I didn't work it out for a day or two. I didn't even think about it. Then I did. Have your cake and eat it! I never understood that saying before, now I do. Your cake is still in your hand even though you've just eaten it. My parents followed the teachings and they obeyed the elders and did everything that was right and can expect to be admitted to the earthly paradise — and at the same time they can have me alive without any of us being disassociated. Transfused, but not our fault! Blame the judge, blame the godless system, blame what we sometimes call 'the world'. What a relief! We've still got our son even though we said he must die. Our son the cake!

I can't work out what to make of this. Was it a fraud? It was a turning point for me. I'm cutting a long story short. When they brought me home I moved the Bible out of my room, I symbolically put it out in the hall face down on a chair and I told my parents that I won't be going near Kingdom Hall again, and they can disassociate me all they like. We've had some terrible rows. Mr Crosby has been round to talk sense into me. No chance. I've been writing to you because I really needed to talk to you, I need to hear your calm voice and have your clear mind discuss this with me. I feel you've brought me close to something else, something really beautiful and deep but I don't really know what it is. You never told me what you believed in, but I loved it when you came and sat with me and we did 'The Salley Gardens'. I still look at that poem every day. I love being 'young and foolish' and if it wasn't for you I'd be neither, I'd be dead! I wrote you lots of stupid letters and I think about you all the time and really want to see you and talk again. I daydream about us, impossible wonderful fantasies, like we go on a journey together round the world in a ship and we have cabins next door to each other and we walk up and down on the deck talking all day.

My Lady, will you please write to me, just a few words to say that you've read this letter and that you don't hate me for writing it.

Yours,
Adam Henry
PS I forgot to say that I'm getting stronger all the time.

★ ★ ★

She did not reply, or rather, she did not post the note it took her almost an hour that evening to compose. In her fourth and final draft she thought she was friendly enough, glad to learn that he was home and feeling better, pleased that he had good memories of her visit. She advised him to be loving towards his parents. It was normal in one's teenage years to question the beliefs one had grown up with, but one should do it in a respectful manner. She finished by saying, although it was not true, that she had been 'tickled' by the idea of the boat trip round the world. She added that when she was young, she'd had dreams of escape just like his own. This wasn't true either, for she had been too ambitious, even at sixteen, too hungry for good grades on her essays to think of running off. Teenage visits to her Newcastle cousins had been her only adventures. When she looked at her short letter a day later, it wasn't the friendliness that struck her, it was the coolness, the dud advice, the threefold impersonal use of 'one', the manufactured recollection. She reread his and was touched again by its innocence and warmth. Better to send nothing at all than cast him down. If she changed her mind, she could write later.

The time was approaching when she would be on circuit, visiting English cities and the old Assize towns in the company of another judge whose field was criminal and civil law. She would hear cases that otherwise would need to travel to the law courts in London. She would stay in specially maintained lodgings, impressive town houses of historical and architectural interest where, in certain cases, the cellars were legendary and the housekeeper was likely to be a decent cook. It was customary to be invited to a dinner given by the high sheriff. Then she and her fellow judge would return the compliment at the lodgings and invite notable or interesting types (there was a distinction) from the locality. The bedrooms were far grander than her own, the beds wider, the sheets of finer weave. In happier days, there was, for a securely married woman, guilty and sensuous pleasure in such unshared accommodation. Now, she longed to be gone from the silent and solemn *pas de deux* at home. And first stop was her favourite English city.

One morning in early September, a week before she began her journey, she received a second letter. Her concern was greater this time, even before she opened it, for the blue envelope lay on the doormat in the hallway at home, along with circulars and an electricity bill. No address, only her name. Easy enough for Adam Henry to wait outside in the Strand or in Carey Street and follow her at a distance.

Jack had already left for work. She took the letter into the kitchen and sat down with the remains of her breakfast.

My Lady,
I don't even know what I wrote because I didn't keep a copy but it's okay that you didn't reply. I still need to talk to you. Here's my news — big rows with my parents, fantastic to be back at school, feeling better, feeling happy and then sad and then happy again. Sometimes the idea of having a stranger's blood inside me makes me sick, like drinking someone's saliva. Or worse. I can't get rid of the idea that transfusion is wrong but I don't care any more. I've got so many questions for you but I'm not even sure you remember me. You must have had dozens of cases since me and loads of choices you've

had to make about other people. I feel jealous! I wanted to talk to you in the street, come up and tap you on the shoulder. I couldn't do it because I'm a coward. I thought you might not recognise me. You don't have to reply to this one either — which means I wish you would. Please don't worry, I'm not wanting to harass you or anything like that. I just feel the top of my head has exploded. All kinds of things are coming out!

    Yours sincerely,
    Adam Henry

Immediately, she emailed Marina Greene to ask if she could find time, as a matter of routine follow-up, to visit the boy and report back. By the end of the day she had a reply. Marina had met Adam that afternoon at his school, where he was starting an extra term to prepare for exams before Christmas. She spent half an hour with him. He had put on weight, there was colour in his cheeks. He was lively, even 'funny and mischievous'. There was some trouble at home, mostly over religious differences with his parents, but she thought there was nothing unusual in that. Separately, the headmaster told her that Adam had done well in his time after hospital to catch up with his essays. His teachers thought he was turning in excellent work. Contributing well in class, no behavioural issues. All in all, it had turned out well. Reassured, Fiona decided against writing to him.

A week later, on the Monday morning she was to leave for the north-east of England, there occurred a minuscule shift along the marital fault lines, a movement as near-imperceptible as continental drift. It was unspoken, unacknowledged. Later, when she was on the train, thinking it through, the moment appeared to straddle the borders of the real and the imagined. Could she trust her recollection? It was seven thirty when she had come into the kitchen. Jack was standing by the counter with his back to her, pouring beans into the grinder. Her suitcase was in the hall and she was preoccupied with gathering up a few last documents. As usual, she was reluctant to be in a confined space with him. She picked up a scarf from the back of a chair and left to continue her search in the sitting room.

Some minutes later she came back. He was taking a jug of milk from the microwave. They were particular about their morning coffee and over the years their tastes had converged. They liked it strong, in tall white thin-lipped cups, filtered from high-grade Colombian beans, with warmed, not hot, milk. Still with his back to her, he poured milk into his coffee, then he turned with the raised cup only slightly extended towards her. There was nothing in his expression to suggest he was offering it to her, and she didn't shake or nod her head. Their eyes met briefly. Then he set the cup down on the deal table and pushed it an inch or so towards her. In itself, this need not have meant much at all, for in their tense prowling around each other they remained pointedly courteous, as though each was trying to outdo the other in appearing reasonable, blamelessly above rancour. It would not have done to make a pot of coffee only large enough for oneself. But there are ways of setting down a cup on a table, from the peremptory clip of china on wood to a sensitive noiseless positing, and there are ways of accepting a cup, which she did smoothly, in slow motion, and after she had taken one sip she didn't wander off, or not immediately, as she might have on any other morning. A few silent seconds passed, and then it seemed that this was as far as they were prepared to go, that the moment contained too much for them and to attempt more would have set them back. He turned away from her to reach a cup for himself, and she turned away from him to go and fetch something from the bedroom. They moved a little more slowly than usual, perhaps even reluctantly.

By early afternoon she was in Newcastle. A driver was at the ticket barrier to take her to the law courts on the Quayside. Nigel Pauling was waiting for her by the judges' entrance and led her to her room. He had driven up from London that morning with court papers and her robes — the full fig, as he put it — because she would be sitting in the Queen's Bench as well as in the Family Division. The clerk of the court came in to make a formal welcome, then the listings officer paid a visit and together they went through the cases listed for the days ahead.

There were other minor matters and it was not until four that she was free to leave. The forecast was of a rainstorm sweeping in from the south-west in the early evening. She told her driver to wait and took a stroll on the broad pavement by the river, under the Tyne Bridge and along Sandhill, past new pavement cafés, and floral displays by solid mercantile buildings with classical facades. She went up the stairs to Castle Garth and paused at the top to look back towards the river. She had a taste for this kind of exuberant tangle of muscular cast iron, of post-industrial steel and glass, of old warehouses teased out of decrepitude into a fantasy youth of coffee shops and bars. She had a history with Newcastle and felt at ease here. In her teens she had come several times during her mother's recurrent illnesses to stay with her favourite cousins. Uncle Fred, a dentist, was the wealthiest man she had ever known. Aunt Simone taught French at a grammar school. The house was pleasingly chaotic, a liberation from her mother's airless polished domain in Finchley. Her cousins, both girls about her age, were jolly and wild and forced her out in the evenings on terrifying missions that included drink and four dedicated musicians with waist-length hair and droopy moustaches, who looked debauched but turned out to be kind. Her parents would have been amazed and distraught to know that their studious sixteen-year-old daughter was a familiar face in certain clubs, drank cherry brandies and rum and Cokes, and had taken her first lover. And along with her cousins, she was a faithful groupie, tolerated as a novice roadie for an under-equipped, unpaid blues band, helping to haul amps and drum kit into the back of a rusty van that was always breaking down. She often tuned the guitars. Her emancipation had much

137

to do with the fact that her visits were infrequent and never longer than three weeks. If she'd stayed longer — never a possibility — she might even have been allowed to sing the blues. She might have married Keith, the lead singer and harmonica player with a withered arm whom she shyly adored.

Uncle Fred moved his practice south when she was eighteen and the affair with Keith ended in tears and some love poems she didn't send. This was an encounter with risk and riotous fun she was never to experience again, and it remained inseparable from her idea of Newcastle. It could not have been replicated in London, the seat of her professional ambitions. Over many years she had been back to the north-east on various pretexts, and four occasions on circuit. It always lifted her spirits to approach the city within sight of Stephenson's High Level Bridge over the Tyne, and to arrive like her excited teenage self, stepping off the train at Newcastle Central under the three great curved arches of John Dobson's creation, and to come out by way of Thomas Prosser's extravagant neoclassical porte cochère. It was her dentist uncle, rolling up to greet her in his green Jaguar with her impatient cousins on board, who had taught her to appreciate the station and the town's architectural treasures. She had never lost the impression of having come abroad to find herself in a Baltic city-state of curious optimism and pride. The air was keener, the light a spacious luminescent grey, the natives friendly, but with sharper edges, self-conscious, or self-ironic like actors in a comedy.

Alongside theirs, her southern accent sounded constricted and contrived. If, as Jack insisted, geology shaped the variety of British character and destinies, then the locals were granite, she was crumbly limestone brash. But in her girlish infatuation with the city, her cousins, the band and her first boyfriend, she believed she could change, become truer, more real, become a Geordie. Years later, the memory of that ambition could still make her smile. But it continued to haunt her whenever she returned, a hazy notion of renewal, of undiscovered potential in another life, even as her sixtieth birthday approached.

★　★　★

The car she reclined in was a 1960s Bentley, her destination, Leadman Hall, set a mile inside its park, which she was entering now by the lodge-house gates. Soon she passed a cricket ground, then an avenue of beeches, already agitating in a strengthening breeze, then a lake choked with greenery. The hall, in the Palladian style, recently painted a too brilliant white, had twelve bedrooms and nine staff to accommodate and serve two High Court judges on circuit. Pevsner had mildly approved of the orangery, and nothing else. Only a bureaucratic anomaly had preserved Leadman's from the cost-cutter's blade, but the game was almost up, this was its final year as far as the judiciary was concerned. The hall, rented a few weeks a year from a local family with historic coal-mining interests, served mostly as a conference centre and wedding venue. Its golf course, tennis courts and heated outdoor pool were, it was now realised, unnecessary luxuries for hard-working judges passing through. From next year, a local taxi firm would be supplying a roomy Vauxhall to replace the Bentley. Accommodation would be in a central Newcastle hotel. Judges on circuit for the Criminal Division, who occasionally sent down for long periods local men with fearsome relatives, rather preferred the seclusion of a grand house. But no one could make the case for Leadman's without sounding self-interested.

Pauling was waiting with the housekeeper on the gravel by the main door. For this final visit he wanted to create a sense of occasion. He stepped up to the car's rear door with an ironic flourish and a click of heels. As usual the housekeeper was new. This one was Polish, a young woman barely in her twenties, Fiona thought, but her gaze was level and cool and she took the judge's largest piece of luggage in a firm grip before Pauling could get to it. Side by side, clerk and housekeeper led the way to the room on the first floor Fiona considered hers. It was at the front of the house, with three tall windows facing towards the beech avenue and part of the weedy lake. Beyond the thirty-foot bedroom was a sitting room with writing desk. The bathroom, however, was along a corridor and down three carpeted steps. The last time Leadman's was modernised, the general proliferation of lavatories and showers had yet to begin.

The storm arrived as she returned from her bath. She stood at the centre window in a dressing gown watching squalls of rain, tall ghostly shapes, hurrying across the fields, which for seconds were lost to view. She saw the topmost branch of one of the nearer beeches snap and begin to fall, upend itself and swing as it was held by lower branches, then plunge again, become entangled, then, freed by the wind, hit the drive with a crack. Almost as loud as the rain hissing against the gravel was the moaning tumult in the guttering. She turned on the lights and began to dress. She was already ten minutes late for sherry in the drawing room.

Four men in dark suits and ties, each holding a gin and tonic, ceased talking and rose from their armchairs as she entered. A waiter in a stiff white jacket mixed her drink while her colleague, Caradoc Ball from the Queen's Bench, doing the criminal list, introduced her to the others, a professor of jurisprudence, a man whose business was in fibre optics and someone working for the government in coastline conservation. All were connected with Ball in some way. She had not invited guests for the first evening. There followed some obligatory conversation about the violent weather. Then, a digression on how people over fifty and all Americans still inhabited a Fahrenheit world. Next, on how British newspapers, for maximum impact, reported cold weather in Celsius, hot in Fahrenheit. All the while, she was wondering why the young man bending low over a trolley in the corner of the room was taking so long. He brought her drink just as the long-ago transition to decimal currency was being recalled.

She already knew from Ball that he was

in Newcastle for the retrial of a murder case in which a man was alleged to have bludgeoned his mother to death at her home because of her ill-treatment of her youngest child, the half-sister of the accused. No murder weapon was found and the DNA evidence was inconclusive. The defence's case was that the woman had been killed by an intruder. The trial had collapsed when it was discovered that one juror had revealed to the others information he had got from the internet through his phone. He had found a five-year-old tabloid story about the accused man's previous conviction for violent assault. In the new age of digital access, something had to be done to 'clarify' matters for juries. The professor of jurisprudence had lately been making a submission to the Law Commission, and this must have been the conversation that Fiona interrupted when she came into the room. Now it resumed. The fibre-optic man was asking how one could ever prevent juries from looking things up in the privacy of their homes, or from getting a family member to do it for them. Relatively simple, was the professor's point. Juries would police themselves. They would be obliged, under threat of a custodial sentence, to report anyone discussing matters not presented in court. Two years maximum for doing so, six months maximum for failing to report a breach. The commission would deliver its conclusions next year.

Just then the butler came in to invite them to the dinner table. Though he could hardly have been out of his thirties, his face was deadly pale, as though dusted in powder. As white as an aspirin, she had once heard a rural French lady say. But he didn't seem to be ill, for his presentation was impersonal and assured. While he stood to one side, attentively stooped, they finished their drinks and followed Fiona through a set of double doors to the dining room. The table, which could have seated thirty guests, was set for five at one lonely end. The room was lined with wood panels, painted over in near-fluorescent orange with evenly spaced stencilled flamingos. The diners were now on the north side of the house, where the wind blew and the three sash windows shook and rumbled. The air was chilly and damp. There was a dusty bouquet of dried flowers in the fireplace. The butler explained that it had been blocked up many years ago, but he would bring in an electric fan heater. They considered the placement and after a hiatus of polite dithering, it was agreed that, for the sake of symmetry, Fiona should sit at the head.

So far she had barely spoken. The pale butler went round with a white wine. Two waiters brought in kipper pâté and thin toast. Immediately to her left was the conservation expert, Charlie, fifty-ish, plump, genially bald. While the other three continued to talk about juries, he politely asked about her work. Resigned to a round of necessary small talk, she spoke in general terms about the Family Division. But Charlie wanted detail. What sort of thing would she rule on tomorrow? She felt happier talking of a particular case. A local authority wanted to take two children, a boy of two and girl of four, into care. The mother was an alcoholic, also addicted to amphetamines. She suffered psychotic episodes during which she believed herself to be spied on by light bulbs. She was no longer able to look after herself or her children. The estranged father had been absent and now had turned up to claim that he and his girlfriend could do the caring. He too had drug problems, as well as a criminal record, but he had rights. A social worker would give evidence in court tomorrow on his suitability as a parent. The grandparents on the mother's side loved the children, were competent and wanted to take them on, but they had no rights. The local authority, whose children service had been criticised in an official report, opposed the grandparents for reasons that were not yet clear. The three parties, mother, father and grandparents, were bitterly divided among themselves. Another complication was that there were contradictory views of the four-year-old. One paediatric expert said that she had special needs, another brought in by the grandparents believed that, though she was disturbed by her mother's behaviour and underweight because of irregular meals, her development was normal.

There were, she said, many other such cases listed for the week. Charlie put his hand to his forehead and closed his eyes. What a mess. If he had to wade in and take a decision tomorrow morning about just one case like that, he would be up all night, chewing his fingernails and abusing the honour bar in the drawing room. She asked him why he was here. He had come from Whitehall to persuade a group of farmers on the coast to join with some local environmental organisations and allow their pastureland to be overrun by seawater in order to return it to salt marshes. This was by far the best and cheapest form of defence against coastal flooding, wonderful for wildlife, especially birds, and good for small-scale tourism too. But there was strong opposition from parts of the agricultural sector, even though the farmers would be well compensated. All day he had been shouted down in meetings. The story was going round that the scheme was compulsory. They wouldn't believe him when he said it wasn't. He was seen as a representative of central government, and farmers were angry about all kinds of other issues which were not his department. Afterwards, he had been jostled in a corridor. A man 'half my age and twice my strength' had gripped his lapel and muttered something in the local accent that he had not understood. Just as well. Tomorrow he would go back and try again. He was sure he'd get there in the end.

Well, that sounded to her like a special circle of hell and she'd settle for a psychotic mother any day. They were chuckling over this when they became aware that the other three had abandoned their conversation and were listening.

Caradoc Ball, who was an old school friend of Charlie, said, 'I hope you realise just how distinguished a judge this is that you're talking to. I'm sure you remember the Siamese twins affair.'

Everyone did, and as the plates were cleared

and the *boeuf en croûte* and Château Latour distributed, they talked of and asked her questions about that famous case. She told them everything they wanted to know. Everyone had a view, but since it was the same view, they soon moved on to discuss the passion and competition for the story in the papers. It was a short step to a gossipy round-up of the latest performances in front of the Leveson Inquiry. They finished the beef. In prospect, according to the menu card, was bread and butter pudding. Soon, Fiona guessed, they would be arguing about the folly or wisdom of the West not sending its armies into Syria. Caradoc was unstoppable on the subject. And so it turned out, this theme was just being introduced by him when they became aware of voices echoing in the hall outside. Pauling and the white-faced butler came in, paused on the threshold, then approached her.

The butler stood aside, looking displeased as Pauling, after nodding an apology to the company, leaned over by her chair and said softly into her ear, 'My Lady, I'm sorry to interrupt, but I'm afraid there's a matter that needs your immediate attention.'

She dabbed her lips with her napkin and stood. 'Excuse me, gentlemen.'

Expressionless, they all rose as she preceded the two men across the room. When she was outside she said to the butler, 'We're still waiting for that fan heater.'

'I'll fetch it now.'

There was something peremptory in his manner as he turned away, and she looked at her clerk with raised eyebrows.

But he simply said, 'It's this way.'

She followed him across the hallway and into what had once been a library. The shelves were filled with junk-shop books, the sort that hotels bought by the yard to lend atmosphere.

Pauling said, 'It's that Jehovah's Witness lad, Adam Henry. Do you remember, from the transfusion case? He seems to have followed you here. He's been walking through the rain, completely drenched. They wanted to turn him out, but I thought you should know first.'

'Where is he now?'

'In the kitchen. It's warmer there.'

'Better bring him in.'

As soon as Pauling had left she got up and walked slowly around the room, conscious that her heart rate had increased. If she'd answered his letters she wouldn't have been facing this now. Facing what? Unnecessary involvement with a case that was closed. And more than that. But there was no time to consider. She heard footsteps approaching.

The door swung open and Pauling ushered in the boy. She had never seen him out of bed and was surprised by how tall he was, well over six feet. He wore his school clothes, grey flannel trousers, grey sweater, white shirt, a flimsy school blazer, all soaked through, and his hair was untidy from being rubbed dry. A small backpack drooped from his hand. A pathetic touch was the Leadman's tea towel, printed with a collage of local beauty spots, draped across his shoulders for warmth.

The clerk hovered in the doorway while the boy took a couple of steps into the room and stopped close to where she stood and said, 'I'm truly sorry.'

In those first moments it was easier to conceal a confusion of feeling behind a motherly tone. 'You look frozen. We'd better have them bring that heater in here.'

'I'll bring it myself,' Pauling said, and left.

'Well,' she said after a silence. 'How on earth did you find me here?'

Another evasion, to ask how rather than why, but at this stage, while his presence was still a shock, she couldn't face knowing what he wanted from her.

His recitation was sober. 'I followed you in a taxi to King's Cross, got on your train, no idea where you'd get off so I had to buy a ticket to Edinburgh. At Newcastle, I followed you out through the station entrance, ran after your limo, then I lost it, so I took a guess and asked people where the law courts were. As soon as I got there I saw your car.'

She watched him as he spoke, taking in the transformation. No longer thin, but still slender. New strength about the shoulders and arms. Same long delicately structured face, the brown cheekbone mole nearly invisible against a complexion darkened by young health. Mere traces of the purple pouches under the eyes. Lips full and moist, eyes in this light too black for colour. Even when he was trying to be apologetic, he appeared too vivid, too hungry for the minutiae of his own explanation. As he looked away from

148

her to order in his thoughts the sequence of events, she wondered if this was what her mother would have called an old-fashioned face. A meaningless idea. Everyone's notion of the face of a Romantic poet, a cousin of Keats or Shelley.

'I waited a really long time, then you came out and I followed you through the town and back down towards the river and watched you get in the car. It took me more than an hour, but eventually I found a site on my phone that mentioned where the judges stay, so I hitched a lift, got dropped off on the main road, climbed over the wall to avoid going past that gatehouse and walked up the drive in the storm. I waited round the back by the old stables for ages, wondering what to do, and then someone saw me. I really am sorry. I . . . '

Pauling, flushed and irritable, came in with the heater. He may have needed to wrench it from the butler's possession. They watched as the clerk went down on all fours with a grunt, and partly disappeared under a side table to get to a socket. After he had reversed out and stood, he placed his hands on the young man's shoulders and steered him into the flow of warm air. Before he left he said to Fiona, 'I'll be right outside.'

When they were alone she said, 'Shouldn't I think there's something spooky about you following me home, and then here?'

'Oh no! Please don't think that. It's not like that.' He cast around with an impatient movement, as though an explanation were written somewhere in the room. 'Look, you saved my life. And it's not only that. My dad tried to keep

149

it from me, but I read your judgment. You said you wanted to protect me from my religion. Well you have. I'm saved!'

He laughed at his own joke and she said, 'I didn't save you so that you could stalk me the length of the country.'

Just then a fixed component of the fan heater must have expanded into the orbit of a moving part, for a regular clunking sound filled the room. It grew louder, then diminished, then steadied. She felt a rush of irritation with the whole establishment. A fake. A dump. How had she not noticed before?

The moment passed and she said, 'Do your parents know where you are?'

'I'm eighteen. I can be where I like.'

'I don't care how old you are. They'll be worried.'

He gave a gasp of adolescent exasperation and set his backpack down on the floor. 'Look, My Lady — '

'Enough of that. It's Fiona.' As long as she could keep him in his place she felt better.

'I wasn't meaning to be sarcastic or anything.'

'Fine. What about your parents?'

'Yesterday I had this huge row with my dad. We've had a few since I came out of hospital, but this one was really big, both shouting, and I told him everything I thought about his stupid religion, not that he was listening. In the end I walked out. I went up to my room and packed my bag, got my savings and said goodbye to my mum. Then I left.'

'You must phone her now.'

'No need. I texted her last night from where I was staying.'

'Text her again.'

He looked at her, both surprised and disappointed.

'Come on. Tell her you're safe and happy in Newcastle and you'll write again tomorrow. Then we'll talk.'

She stood a few paces off and watched as his long thumbs danced across a virtual keyboard. In seconds the phone was back in his pocket.

'There,' he said, looking at her expectantly, as though she were the one who was to give an account of herself.

She crossed her arms. 'Adam, why are you here?'

His gaze slid away and he hesitated. He was not going to tell her, or not directly.

'Look, I'm not the same person. When you came to see me I really was ready to die. It's amazing that people like you could waste your time on me. I was such an idiot!'

She gestured towards two wooden chairs by an oval walnut table and they sat facing each other across it. The ceiling light, a factory-stressed rustic wheel of stained wood bearing four energy-conserving lamps, cast down from one side a ghastly white glow. It heightened the contours of his cheekbones and lips, and picked out the fine twin ridges of his philtrum. It was a beautiful face.

'I didn't think you were an idiot.'

'But I was. Whenever the doctors and nurses tried to talk me round, I felt sort of noble and

151

heroic telling them to leave me alone. I was pure and good. I loved it that they couldn't understand how profound I was. I was really pumped up. I liked it that my parents and the elders were proud. At night when no one was around I rehearsed making a video, like suicide bombers do. I was going to do it on my phone. I wanted it on the television news and at my funeral. I made myself cry in the dark, imagining them carrying my coffin past my parents, past my school friends and teachers, the whole congregation, the flowers, the wreaths, the sad music, everyone weeping, everyone proud of me and loving me. Honestly, I was an idiot.'

'And where was God?'

'Behind everything. These were his instructions I was obeying. But it was mostly about the delicious adventure I was on, how I would die beautifully and be adored. This girl I know at school had anorexia three years ago, when she was fifteen. Her dream was of wasting away to nothing — like a dried leaf in the wind, was what she said, just fading gently into death and everyone pitying her and blaming themselves afterwards for not understanding her. Same sort of thing.'

Now he was sitting she remembered him in hospital, leaning against the pillows among the teenage debris. It wasn't his sickliness that came back to her, it was the eagerness, the vulnerable innocence. Even the word anorexia on his lips sounded like a hopeful jaunt. He had taken from his pocket a narrow strip of green cloth, something torn from a lining perhaps, which he rolled and rubbed between forefinger and thumb like worry beads.

'So this wasn't so much about your religion then. More about your feelings.'

He raised both hands. 'My feelings came out of my religion. I was doing God's will, and you and all the rest were plain wrong. How could I have got into such a mess without being a Witness?'

'Sounds like your anorexic friend managed it.'

'Yeah, well, actually, anorexia's a bit like religion.'

When she looked sceptical he improvised. 'Oh, you know, wanting to suffer, loving the pain and sacrifice, thinking that everyone's watching and caring and that the whole universe is all about you. And your weight!'

She couldn't help herself, she laughed at the po-faced self-ironic afterthought. He grinned at his unexpected success in amusing her.

They heard voices and footsteps in the hallway as the guests left the dining room and crossed to the sitting room for coffee. Then a staccato bark of laughter close to the library door. The boy tensed at the possibility of an interruption and they sat in conspiratorial silence, waiting for the sounds to recede. Adam was staring down at his clasped hands on the polished grain of the table. She wondered at all the hours of his childhood and teenage years, of praying, hymns, sermons, and various constraints that she could never know about, at the tight and loving community that had sustained him until it had almost killed him.

'Adam, I'm asking you again. Why are you here?'

'To thank you.'

'There are easier ways.'

He sighed impatiently as he replaced the strip of cloth in his pocket. For a moment she thought he was getting ready to leave.

'Your visit was one of the best things that ever happened.' Then, quickly, 'My parents' religion was a poison and you were the antidote.'

'I don't remember talking against your parents' faith.'

'You didn't. You were calm, you listened, you asked questions, you made some comments. That was the point. It's this thing you have. It added up to something. You didn't have to say it. A way of thinking and talking. If you don't know what I mean, go and listen to the elders. And when we did our song . . . '

She said briskly, 'Are you still playing the violin?'

He nodded.

'And the poetry?'

'Yes, lots. But I hate the stuff I was writing before.'

'Well, you're good. I know you'll write something wonderful.'

She saw the dismay in his eyes. She was distancing herself, playing the solicitous aunt. She went a couple of steps back through the conversation, wondering why she was so anxious not to disappoint him.

'But your teachers must have been very different from the elders.'

He shrugged. 'I don't know.' He added by way of explanation, 'The school was enormous.'

'And what is this thing I'm supposed to have?' She said it gravely, allowing no hint of irony.

The question didn't embarrass him. 'When I saw my parents crying like that, really crying, crying and sort of hooting for joy, everything collapsed. But this is the point. It collapsed into the truth. Of course they didn't want me to die! They love me. Why didn't they say that, instead of going on about the joys of heaven? That's when I saw it as an ordinary human thing. Ordinary and good. It wasn't about God at all. That was just silly. It was like a grown-up had come into a room full of kids who are making each other miserable and said, Come on, stop all the nonsense, it's teatime! You were the grown-up. You knew all along but you didn't say. You just asked questions and listened. All of life and love that lie ahead of him — that's what you wrote. That was your 'thing'. And my revelation. From 'The Salley Gardens' onwards.'

Still grave in her manner she said, 'The top of your head has exploded.'

He laughed with delight at being quoted in turn. 'Fiona, I can almost get through this piece by Bach without a mistake. I can do the theme from *Coronation Street*. I've been reading Berryman's *Dream Songs*. I'm going to be in a play, and I've got to do all my exams before Christmas. And thanks to you I'm full of Yeats!'

'Yes,' she said quietly.

He leaned forwards on his elbows, dark eyes gleaming in the awful light, his whole face appearing to tremble with anticipation, with unbearable appetite.

She considered for a moment, then said in a whisper, 'Wait here.'

She stood up, hesitated, and seemed about to change her mind and sit down. But she turned away from him, crossed the room, stepped out into the hall. Pauling was standing a few paces off, pretending to be interested in the pages of the visitors' book resting on a marble-topped table. In a low voice she gave rapid instructions, returned to the library and closed the door behind her.

Adam had pulled the tea towel away from his shoulders and was examining the collage of local attractions. As she returned to her seat he said, 'I've never heard of any of these places.'

'There's lots to discover.'

When the effects of the interruption had dissipated she said, 'So you've lost your faith.'

He seemed to squirm. 'Yes, perhaps. I don't know. I think I'm frightened of saying it out loud. I don't know where I am really. I mean, the thing is, once you take a step back from the Witnesses, you might as well go all the way. Why replace one tooth fairy with another?'

'Perhaps everyone needs tooth fairies.'

He smiled forgivingly. 'I don't think you mean that.'

She succumbed to her habit of summarising the views of others. 'You saw your parents crying and you're confused because you suspect their love for you is greater than their belief in God or the afterlife. You need to get away. Perfectly natural in someone your age. Perhaps you'll go to university. That will help. But I still don't understand what you're doing here. And more to the point, what you're about to do now. Where are you going to go?'

This second question troubled him more. 'I've got an aunt in Birmingham. My mother's sister. She'll have me for a week or two.'

'She's expecting you?'

'Sort of.'

She was about to make him send another text, when he extended his hand across the table, and just as quickly she withdrew hers onto her lap.

He couldn't bear to look at her or be looked at as he spoke. He put his hands to his forehead, shading his eyes. 'This is my question. When you hear it you'll think it's so stupid. But please don't just reject it. Please say you'll think about it.'

'Well?'

He spoke to the table's surface. 'I want to come and live with you.'

She waited for more. She could never have anticipated such a request. But now, it seemed obvious.

He still could not meet her eye. He spoke quickly as though embarrassed by his own voice. He had thought it all out. 'I could do odd jobs for you, housework, errands. And you could give me reading lists, you know, everything you think I should know about . . . '

He had stalked her through the country, through the streets, walked through a storm to ask her. It was a logical extension of his fantasy of a long sea voyage with her, of their talking all day as they paced the rolling deck. Logical and insane. And innocent. The silence wound itself around them and bound them. Even the clunking of the fan heater appeared to recede, and

157

there were no sounds from beyond the room. He continued to protect his face from her. She stared at the whorls of his healthy young dark brown hair, now completely dry and shining.

She said gently, 'You know that isn't possible.'

'I wouldn't get in the way, I mean, with you and your husband.' Finally, he removed his hands and looked at her. 'You know, like a sort of lodger. When I've finished my exams I could get a job and pay you some rent.'

She saw the spare room and its twin single beds, the teddies and other animals in the wicker basket, the toy cupboard so crammed that one door would not close. She coughed abruptly and stood, and went the length of the room to the window and made a show of looking out into the dark. At last, without turning, she said, 'We only have one spare room and a lot of nephews and nieces.'

'You mean that's your only objection?'

There was a tap on the door and Pauling came in. 'Here in two minutes, My Lady,' he said, and left.

She came away from the window and went back towards Adam and stooped to pick up his backpack from the floor.

'My clerk will go with you in a taxi, first to the station to buy you a ticket to Birmingham tomorrow morning and then to a hotel close by.'

After a pause he got slowly to his feet and took the bag from her. Despite his height, he looked like a small child in shock.

'Is that it then?'

'I'd like you to promise me you'll contact your

mother again before you get on the train. Tell her where you'll be.'

He didn't reply. She handed him towards the door and they went out into the hall. No one in sight. Caradoc Ball and his guests were settled in the drawing room behind closed doors. She left Adam waiting by the library while she went to her room to get money from her handbag. On her way back, she saw the whole scene from her elevated position at the top of the grand staircase. The front door was open and the butler was talking to the driver. Behind him, below the portico steps, was the taxi, door open to release the cheery swooping sounds of Arabic orchestral music. Her clerk was crossing the hall at a pace, presumably to prevent the butler creating a problem. As for Adam Henry, he was still by the library entrance, pressing the bag in his arms against his chest. By the time she reached him, the butler, the driver and the clerk were outside on the gravel by the car discussing, she hoped, a suitable hotel.

The boy started to say, 'But we haven't even — ' and she raised a hand to shush him.

'You must go.'

Lightly, she took the lapel of his thin jacket between her fingers and drew him towards her. Her intention was to kiss him on the cheek, but as she reached up and he stooped a little and their faces came close, he turned his head and their lips met. She could have drawn back, she could have stepped right away from him. Instead, she lingered, defenceless before the moment. The sensation of skin on skin obliterated any possibility of choice.

159

If it was possible to kiss chastely full on the lips, this was what she did. A fleeting contact, but more than the idea of a kiss, more than a mother might give her grown-up son. Over in two seconds, perhaps three. Time enough to feel in the softness of his lips that overlay their suppleness, all the years, all the life, that separated her from him. As they withdrew, a slight adhesion of skin might have drawn them back together. But there were approaching footsteps on the gravel and on the stone steps outside. She let go of his lapel and said again, 'You must go.'

He picked up his backpack, which he had dropped to the floor, and followed her across the hall and out into the fresh night air. At the foot of the steps the driver gave a friendly salute and opened the taxi's rear door. The music had been turned off. She had intended to give the cash to Adam, but in a sudden pointless change of mind, she handed it to Pauling instead. He nodded and grimaced as he took the thin roll of notes. With a brusque movement of his shoulders, Adam seemed to shake himself free of all of them and ducked into the back seat and sat with the bag on his lap, staring straight ahead. Already beginning to regret what she had set in train, she moved around the car in order to exchange a last look with him. He was surely aware of her, but he turned his head away. Pauling got in the front beside the driver. The butler closed Adam's door with a dismissive backhand flourish. Shoulders hunched, Fiona hurried up the cracked stone steps as the taxi drew away.

5

She moved on from Newcastle after a week, judgments handed down or delayed pending reports, leaving contented or embittered parties, some of whom had the meagre comfort of leave to appeal. In the case she had described to Charlie at dinner, she granted residence to the grandparents, and allowed supervised weekly contact to the mother and father separately, with a return date set for six months. By then, whoever sat in her place would have the benefit of a progress report on the children's welfare, the parents' promises to attend an addiction programme, and the mother's mental state. The little girl would stay at her school, a Church of England primary, where she was well known. Fiona found the conduct of the local authority's children department in this case to be exemplary.

In the late afternoon of Friday she said her farewells to the court officials. On Saturday morning at Leadman Hall, Pauling loaded the boot of the car with documents in boxes and her robes on hangers. With their personal luggage piled on the back seat, and the judge installed in front, they headed west for Carlisle by way of the Tyne Gap, across the whole width of England, Cheviots to the right, Pennines to the left. But the drama of geology and history were dulled by traffic, its volume, its routines and the road furniture that uniformly defined the British Isles.

They were slowing to walking pace through Hexham, her phone lay idle in her hand and she was thinking, as she had during various interludes all week, of the kiss. What impulsive folly, not to have pulled away. Professional and social madness. In memory, the actual contact, flesh on flesh, tended to extend in time. Then she would try to cut the moment back to a blameless peck on the lips. But that peck soon swelled again, until she no longer knew what it was or what had happened or for how long she had risked disgrace. Caradoc Ball could have stepped out into the hall at any point. Worse, one of his guests, unconstrained by tribal loyalty, might have seen her and told the world. Pauling could have turned back indoors from his conversation with the taxi driver and surprised her. Then the sensitively constructed distance between them that made her work possible would have been destroyed.

She was not prone to wild impulses and she didn't understand her own behaviour. She realised there was much more to confront in her confused mix of feelings, but for now it was the horror of what might have come about, the ludicrous and shameful transgression of professional ethics, that occupied her. The ignominy that could have been all hers. Hard to believe that no one had seen her, that she was leaving the scene of the crime, unscathed. Easier to believe that the truth, hard and dark as a bitter seed, was about to reveal itself: that she had been observed and hadn't noticed. That even now, miles behind her

162

in London, the case was being discussed. That one day soon she'd hear on her phone the hesitant embarrassed voice of a senior colleague. *Ah, Fiona, look, awfully sorry but I'm afraid I should warn you, uh, something's come up.* Then, waiting for her back at Gray's Inn, a formal letter from the Judicial Complaints investigation officer.

She tapped two keys to summon her husband on the phone. In flight from a kiss, running scared for the cover of a married woman of some repute, some solidity. She made the call without thinking, out of habit, barely aware of the state of play between her and Jack. When she heard his tentative hello, the acoustic told her that he was in the kitchen. The radio was playing, Poulenc perhaps. On Saturday mornings they always had, always used to have, a lazy but early breakfast, a spread of papers, muted Radio Three, coffee, warmed *pain aux raisins* from Lamb's Conduit Street. He would be in his paisley silk dressing gown. Unshaven, hair uncombed.

In a careful neutral tone, he asked her if she was all right. When she said 'fine' it surprised her how normal she sounded. She began to improvise with facility, just as Pauling, with a satisfied sigh, remembered a short cut and pulled free of the traffic. Plausible enough in the way of good housekeeping to remind Jack of her return date at the end of the month, and natural, or it had once been, to suggest that on the evening she came home they should go out for a meal together. A nearby restaurant they liked was often booked up in advance. Perhaps he could make a reservation now. He thought it was a good idea. She heard him suppress the surprise in his voice, steering cleanly between warmth and distance. He asked her again if she was all right. He knew her too well, and clearly, she wasn't sounding quite so normal. With lightened emphasis she said she was absolutely fine. They exchanged a few lines about work. The call ended on his cautious goodbye that sounded almost like a question.

But it had worked. She was lifted from paranoid reveries into the actuality of an arrangement, a date, an improving relationship. She felt better defended and altogether more sensible. If there had been a complaint against her, she would have heard it by now. It was good to have phoned and moved matters on from that indefinable breakfast moment. Worth remembering the world was never how she anxiously dreamed it. An hour later, as the car began the slow crawl along the congested A69 into Carlisle, she was absorbed in court papers.

And so it was, two weeks later, her circuit complete and yet more justice dispensed across four northern cities, she faced her husband across a quiet corner table in a Clerkenwell restaurant. A bottle of wine stood between them, but they drank it warily. There was to be no sudden rush to intimacy. They kept away from the subject that might have destroyed them. He spoke to her with an awkward delicacy as though she was some kind of unusual bomb that might go off mid-sentence. She asked about work, about his Virgil book, an introduction and

164

selection, a 'worldwide' textbook for schools and universities which, he touchingly believed, would make his fortune. Nervously, she posed one question after another, aware that she was sounding like an interviewer. She hoped to observe him as though for the first time, see the strangeness in him, as she had many years before, when she fell in love with him. Not easy. His voice, his features were as familiar as her own. His face had a rugged, haunted look. Attractive, of course, but not to her just then. His hands, resting on the table by his glass, were not, she hoped, about to take one of hers.

Towards the end of the meal, when they had exhausted the safer topics, there came a threatening silence. Their appetites were gone, their desserts and half the wine were untouched. Unspoken mutual recrimination troubled them. Still on her mind, his brazen excursion; on his, she presumed, her overblown sense of injury. In a forced tone, he began telling her about a geology lecture he'd been to the night before. It described how the sequence of sedimentary rock strata could be read like a book of the earth's history. To finish, the lecturer allowed himself some speculation. A hundred million years into the future, when much of the oceans had sunk into the earth's mantle and there wasn't enough carbon dioxide in the atmosphere to sustain plants and the surface of the world was lifeless rocky desert, what evidence would a visiting extraterrestrial geologist find of our civilisation? A few feet below the ground a thick dark line in the rock would mark us off from all that had gone before. Condensed into that six-inch sooty layer would be our cities, vehicles, roads, bridges, weapons. Also, all sorts of chemical compounds not found in the previous geological record. Concrete and brick would weather down as easily as limestone. Our finest steel would become a crumbling ferrous stain. A more detailed microscopic examination might reveal a preponderance of pollen from the monotonous grasslands we had made to feed a giant population of livestock. With luck, the geologist might find fossilised bones, even ours. But wild creatures, including all the fish, would barely make up a tenth of the weight of all the sheep and cows. He was bound to conclude that he was looking at the beginning of a mass extinction in which life's variety had started to narrow.

Jack had been speaking for five minutes. He was oppressing her with the weight of meaningless time. The unimaginable desert of years, the inevitable end, animated him. But not her. Bleakness was settling around her. She felt the weight of it on her shoulders and down through her legs. Taking her napkin from her lap, she placed it on the table, a gesture of surrender, and then stood.

He was saying, as though in wonder, 'This is how we're signing our names in the geological record.'

She said, 'I think we should get the bill,' and walked quickly across the restaurant to the Ladies, where she stood in front of the mirror, eyes closed, comb in hand in case someone came in, and drew a few slow deep breaths.

166

The thaw was neither quick nor linear. At first it was a relief, not to be self-consciously avoiding each other around the flat, not to be coldly competing in politeness in that stifling way they had. They ate meals together, began to accept invitations to supper with friends, had conversations — about work mostly. But he still slept in the spare room, and when a nineteen-year-old nephew came to stay, he moved onto the sitting-room couch again.

Late October. The clocks went back, marking the final stretch of an exhausted year, and the darkness closed in. For a few weeks, a new stasis developed between her and Jack and seemed almost as suffocating as before. But she was busy, and too tired in the evenings to begin the demanding conversations that might move them to a new stage. In addition to the usual case load in the Strand, she was chairing a committee on new court procedures, and sat on another to respond to a White Paper on family-law reform. If she had the energy after supper, she practised alone at the piano, in preparation for her rehearsals with Mark Berner. Jack was busy too, filling in for a sick colleague at the university, and at home absorbed in writing the long introduction to his Virgil selection.

She and Berner had been told by the barrister organising the Christmas Revels in the Great Hall that they had been chosen to open the concert. They were to perform for no more than twenty minutes, allowing five minutes maximum for an encore. Enough time for their selection from Berlioz's *Les nuits d'été* and a song by

167

Mahler, one of the *Rückert-Lieder*, 'I am lost to the world'. The Gray's Inn choir would sing some Monteverdi and Bach, followed by a string quartet performing Haydn. A large minority of Gray's Inn benchers spent many evenings a year listening in frowning concentration to chamber music over in Marylebone, at Wigmore Hall. They knew the repertoire. It was said they knew a bad note before it was played. Here, even though there would be wine beforehand and the general atmosphere, at least outwardly, would be forgiving, standards were punitively high for an amateur affair. Sometimes Fiona woke before dawn and wondered if she was up to it this time, whether there was some way she could excuse herself. She thought she lacked the concentration, and the Mahler was difficult. So languorously slow and poised. It would expose her. And the Germanic yearning for oblivion made her uncomfortable. But Mark was burning to perform. Two years before, his marriage had broken up. Now, according to Sherwood Runcie, there was a woman in his life. Fiona guessed that she would be in the audience and Mark was keen to impress her. He had even asked Fiona to learn the pieces by heart, but that, she told him, was beyond her. Only their three or four little encores were committed to memory.

At the end of October she found in the morning post at the Courts of Justice a familiar blue envelope. Pauling was in the room at the time. To conceal her feelings, a mix of excitement and vague fear, she took the letter to the window and pretended an interest in the courtyard below.

168

When Pauling had left, she took from the envelope a single sheet of paper, folded in four, torn across the bottom, on which was an unfinished poem. Its title was in block capitals, underlined twice. 'THE BALLAD OF ADAM HENRY'. The writing was small, the poem was long and ran over the page. No accompanying letter. She glanced at the first verse, failed to take it in, and put it aside. She had a difficult case beginning in half an hour, a set of complicated marital claims and counterclaims that were set to absorb two weeks of her life. Both parties intended to remain exceedingly rich at the expense of the other. This was not the moment for poetry.

Two days passed before she opened the envelope again. It was ten in the evening. Jack was at another lecture on sedimentary layers, or so he said, and she preferred to believe him. She lay on her couch and spread the torn sheet on her lap. It looked to her like doggerel of the birthday card variety. Then she forced herself into a more accepting state of mind. It was a ballad, after all, and he was only eighteen.

THE BALLAD OF ADAM HENRY

I took my wooden cross and dragged it by
the stream.
I was young and foolish and troubled by a
dream
That penitence was folly and burdens were
for fools.
But I'd been told on Sundays to live life by
the rules.

The splinters cut my shoulder, that cross
    was heavy as lead,
My life was narrow and godly and I was
    almost dead,
The stream was merry and dancing and
    sunlight danced around,
But I must keep on walking, with eyes fixed
    on the ground.

Then a fish rose out of the water with
    rainbows on its scales.
Pearls of water were dancing and hung in
    silvery trails.
'Throw your cross in the water if you're
    wanting to be free!'
So I drowned my load in the river in the
    shade of the Judas tree.

I knelt by the banks of that river in a
    wondrous state of bliss
While she leaned upon my shoulder and
    gave the sweetest kiss.
But she dived to the icy bottom where she
    never will be found,
And I was full of tears until I heard the
    trumpets sound.

And Jesus stood on the water and this He
    said to me,
'That fish was the voice of Satan, and you
    must pay the fee.
Her kiss was the kiss of Judas, her kiss
    betrayed my name.
May he

May he what? The last words of the final verse were lost to a skein of spidery lines that looped around second thoughts, to words deleted and reinstated and to other variants with question marks. Rather than attempt to decipher the mess, she read the poem again, then lay back with eyes closed. She minded that he was angry with her, casting her as Satan, and began to daydream a letter to him, knowing that she would never post it, or even write it. Her impulse was to appease him as well as justify herself. She summoned flat ready-made phrases. *I had to send you away, It was in your own best interests, You have your own young life to lead.* Then, more coherently, *Even if we had the room, you could not be our lodger. Such a thing is simply not possible for a judge.* She added, *Adam, I'm not Judas. An old trout perhaps . . .* This last to lighten a fierce self-justifying intent.

Her 'sweetest kiss' had been reckless and she hadn't got away with it, not where he was concerned. But it was only kindness, not to send him a letter. He'd write by return, he'd be at her door and she'd have to turn him away again. She folded the sheet back into its envelope, took it to her bedroom and stored it in the drawer of her bedside table. He would soon move on. Either he had drifted back into religion, or Judas, Jesus and the rest were poetic devices to dramatise her awful behaviour, kissing him then packing him off in a taxi. Whichever it was, Adam Henry was likely to succeed brilliantly at his postponed exams and go to a good university. She would fade in his thoughts, become a minor figure in the progress of his sentimental education.

★   ★   ★

They were in a small bare basement room below Mark Berner's chambers. No one could remember how a Grotrian-Steinweg upright came to be there, no one had claimed it in twenty-five years, no one was minded to move it. There were scratches and cigarette burns on the lid, but the action was good, the tone velvety. Outside it was below freezing, with the season's first inch of snow settling picturesquely on Gray's Inn Square. Here, in what they called the rehearsal room, there was no radiator, but certain downpipes among an array of early Victorian plumbing fixed against one wall gave off a feeble constant heat that happened to keep the instrument in tune. The floor covering, dating from the 1960s, was strips of coffee-stained needlecord that had once been glued down on cement. Now the edges rose rebelliously. It was easy to trip. Lighting was from a dazzling 150-watt bare bulb screwed into the low ceiling. For some while Mark had mentioned getting a shade. Apart from a music stand and piano stool, the only other furniture was a frail kitchen chair, on which their coats and scarves were piled.

Fiona was sitting at the keyboard, hands clasped for warmth on her lap, gazing at the score in front of her, *Les nuits d'été* in an arrangement for piano and tenor voice. Somewhere in her sitting room there was an old recording on vinyl

172

by Kiri Te Kanawa. She hadn't seen it in years. And it wouldn't help them now. They urgently needed to be working on it, because they'd only had two rehearsals so far. But Mark had been in court the day before and was still angry and needed to tell her why. And what he intended to do with his future, for he was leaving the law. He'd had enough. Too sad, too stupid, too wasteful of young lives. An old and empty threat, but as she sat shivering, she felt obliged to hear him out. Even so, she could not stop herself staring at the opening, the 'Villanelle', at the softly repeating chords, pulsing staccato quavers, or imagining the sweet melody, or forming her own prosaic translation of Gautier's first line —

When the new season comes, when the cold has disappeared . . .

Berner's case concerned four young men fighting outside a pub near Tower Bridge with four other young men they happened to meet. All eight had been drinking. Only the first four were arrested and charged. The jury had found them guilty of grievous bodily harm with intent and had accepted the prosecution's argument that the men should be treated on the basis of joint enterprise, that regardless of what each one had done, they should be dealt with equally. They were all in it together. After the verdict, which was a week before sentencing, the judge at Southwark, Christopher Cranham, had advised the men that they should expect serious custodial sentences. At this stage Mark Berner was brought in by anxious relatives of one of the four, Wayne Gallagher. They'd had a whip-round among family and friends and with some clever online crowd-sourcing raised the necessary twenty thousand pounds. The hope was that a QC of repute might speak effectively in mitigation before Gallagher was sentenced. Perfectly competent legal-aid counsel was dismissed, though the instructing solicitor was kept on.

Berner's client was a twenty-three-year-old from Dalston, a somewhat dreamy young man whose chief fault was a degree of passivity. And a failure to keep appointments. His mother was a drunk and a drug addict, the father, with similar problems, was mostly absent from Wayne's childhood, which was one of chaos and neglect. He loved his mother and, he insisted, she loved him. She never hit him. Much of his adolescence was spent being his mother's main carer and he missed a lot of school. He left at sixteen, worked at low-level jobs — in a chicken-plucking factory, as a labourer, in a warehouse, stuffing junk mail through letter boxes. He had never claimed unemployment or housing benefit. Five years earlier, at the age of eighteen, he was maliciously accused of rape by a girl, was held in a young offenders' prison for a couple of weeks, then tagged and put under strict curfew conditions for six months. There was good mobile phone text evidence to prove the sex was consensual, but the police declined to investigate. They had targets to meet in rape cases. Gallagher was just their sort of man. First day of the trial, damning evidence from the accuser's best friend caused the case to collapse. The supposed victim had been hoping for money from the Criminal Injuries Compensation Authority.

She was keen on buying a new Xbox. She had texted her intentions to her friend. Prosecuting counsel was seen to hurl his wig to the floor and mutter 'Stupid girl.'

'Another blot on his record,' Berner said, 'was that back when Gallagher was fifteen he knocked a policeman's helmet off. An idiotic prank. But down on the record as 'assaulting a police officer'.'

Spring has come, my precious. It's the blessed month of lovers.

The barrister was by her left elbow, in front of the music stand. In tight black jeans and black polo-neck sweater he reminded her of an old-fashioned beatnik. An impression only modified by the reading glasses suspended by a cord around his neck.

'D'you know, when Cranham told these lads what to expect, two of them said they wanted to start serving their time immediately. Meek as lambs, turkeys queuing for the oven. So Wayne Gallagher had to go with them, even though he wanted to be with his partner for one last week. She'd just had their baby. So I had to travel all the way out beyond east London to this dump to see him. Thamesmead.'

Fiona turned the page of her score. 'I've been there,' she said. 'Better than most.'

So come onto this mossy bank and let's talk about our wondrous love . . .

'Get this,' Berner said. 'Four London lads. Gallagher, Quinn, O'Rourke, Kelly. Third- or fourth-generation Irish. London accents. All went to the same school. A not-bad comprehensive. The arresting officer saw the names and decided they were tinkers. That's why he didn't bother going after the other four. That's why the CPS went for joint enterprise. They use it for gangs. Very tidy. Nice clean lazy sweep.'

'Mark,' she murmured. 'We should get to work.'

'I'm almost done.'

As it happened, the brawl took place in full view of two CCTV cameras.

'The angles were perfect. You could see everyone. And in muted colours. Pin bloody sharp. Martin Scorsese couldn't have done it better.'

Berner had four days to get his mind around the case, to play and replay the DVD and memorise the shifting movements of an eight-minute brawl caught from two camera positions, to learn by rote every step of his client and the other seven. He watched the men's first contact, on the wide pavement between a shuttered shop and a phone box, an angry verbal exchange, a little pushing, puffed chests, male swagger, the amorphous crowd swaying this way and that, spilling at one point over the kerb, onto the road. A hand gripped a forearm, the heel of another hand shoved a shoulder. Then Wayne Gallagher, who was at the back of the group, raised an arm and, unfortunately for him, struck the first blow, and then another. But his fist was too high, he was too far back, his movements were impeded by the beer can in his other hand. His blows were ineffectual and the man he hit barely noticed. Now the group split untidily in two. At this point, Gallagher, still on the edges, threw his

176

beer can. It was an underarm toss. The intended target brushed away some spots of beer from his lapel. In retribution, one of the other four stepped round and whacked Gallagher hard in the face, splitting his lip and terminating his involvement. He stood still, dazed, then moved away from the fighting, out of the cameras' view.

The fight continued without him. One of the school friends, O'Rourke, stepped in and, with a single blow, floored the one who hit Gallagher. As soon as the man was down, another friend, Kelly, kicked him and fractured his jaw. Half a minute later, a second man went down, and this time it was Quinn who kicked him, breaking his cheek. When the police arrived, the fellow who hit Gallagher got to his feet and ran off to hide in his girlfriend's flat. He was concerned about being arrested and losing his job.

Fiona looked at her watch. 'Mark . . . '

'Almost done, My Lady. The point is, my guy just stood there waiting for the police. Face covered in blood. As much sinned against, et cetera. Bones were broken, so it's GBH. The police charged all four on various counts. But in court the prosecution pushed for joint enterprise and sentence at level 2 GBH on the guidelines, which are five to nine years. Same old story. My client played no part in that violence. He was about to be sentenced for crimes that others committed and with which he wasn't even charged. He'd pleaded not guilty. He should have owned up to an affray, but I wasn't there to advise. Legal aid should have showed the jury the police photo of his bloodied face. In any case, the chap with the fractured jaw refused to file a victim statement. Came to court as a prosecution witness. Said he didn't understand the fuss. Told the judge he hadn't needed treatment, went on holiday to Spain two days after the fight. First couple of days he had to sip his vodka through a straw. End of story — his very words. It's in the court transcript.'

Continuing to listen, she spread her fingers over a chord but did not play it. *Let's head for home, laden with wild strawberries.*

'Obviously, nothing I could do about the jury's verdict. I spoke for seventy-five minutes, trying to detach Wayne from the rest, trying to get the GBH down to level 3. Guidelines are three to five years. Also, made a solid case that the law owed him six months' liberty on the groundless rape charge. Then he would have been within reach of a suspended sentence, which was all this stupidity was worth. The other three legal-aid counsel spoke for ten minutes each for their clients. Cranham summed up. Lazy bastard. Okay, level 3, thank God, but he wouldn't let go of joint enterprise, and completely forgot to address what I'd said about the time the law owed my client. Gave them all two and a half years. Lazy and perverse. But in the gallery the parents of the others were sobbing with relief. They'd been looking at a minimum five years. I'd done them all a favour, I suppose.'

Fiona said, 'The judge used his discretion to go below the guidelines. Count yourself lucky.'

'Not the point, Fiona.'

'Let's start. We've got less than an hour.'

178

'Hear me out. This is my resignation speech. All these guys were in employment. They're taxpayers, for heaven's sake! My man caused no harm. Against the odds, given his background, he was turning out to be a hands-on dad. Kelly was running a youth football team in his spare time. O'Rourke worked at weekends for a cystic fibrosis charity. This wasn't an attack on innocent passers-by. It was a scuffle outside a pub.'

She looked up from the score. 'A broken cheek?'

'All right. A brawl. Between consenting adults. What's the point of stuffing the prisons with these guys? Gallagher swung two harmless punches and tossed a near-empty beer can. Two and a half years. GBH on his record for ever for offences he wasn't charged with. They're sending him to Isis, that young offenders' place, you know, inside the walls of Belmarsh. I've been out there a few times. The website says they have a 'learning academy'. Total crap! I've had clients there in the cells twenty-three hours a day. The courses get cancelled every week. Understaffed, they say. Cranham with his put-on weariness, pretending to be too irritable to listen to anyone. What does he care what happens to these kids? Poured into these dumps, turning sour, learning to be criminals. D'you know what my biggest mistake was?'

'What?'

'I tried to make the point that this was a case of drink and high spirits. The violence was consensual. 'If these four gentlemen had been members of the Bullingdon Club at Oxford they wouldn't be before you now, Your Honour.' On a horrible hunch, when I got home, I looked Cranham up in *Who's Who*. Guess what?'

'Oh God. Mark, you need a holiday.'

'Face it, Fiona. It's bloody class warfare.'

'And in the Family Division it's all champagne and *fraises des bois*.'

Without waiting, she began to play the ten bars of introduction, the softly insistent chords. From the corner of her eye, she saw him putting on his reading glasses. Then the fine tenor voice, obedient to the composer's marking of dolce, swelled sweetly.

Quand viendra la saison nouvelle,
Quand auront disparu les froids . . .

For fifty-five minutes they forgot about the law.

★　★　★

In December, on the day of the concert, she was home from court by six and in a hurry to shower and change. She heard Jack in the kitchen and called a hello to him as she passed on her way to her bedroom. He was bending over by the fridge and grunted in return. Forty minutes later she emerged into the hallway in a black silk dress, and high-heeled shoes of black patent leather. They gave her good leverage with the pedals. Around her neck she wore a simple silver band. Her perfume was Rive Gauche. From the sitting room's rarely touched hi-fi came the sound of

180

piano music, of an old Keith Jarrett record, *Facing You*. The first track. She paused outside her bedroom door to listen. It had been a long time since she'd heard that hesitant partly realised melody. She'd forgotten how smoothly it gathered confidence and leaped into life as the left hand plunged into a strangely altered boogie which became an unstoppable force, like an accelerating steam locomotive. Only a classically trained musician could set his hands free of each other the way Jarrett did. That, at least, was her partial judgement.

Jack was sending her a message, for this was an album, one of three or four, that formed the soundtrack of their long-ago courtship. Those days, post-finals, after the all-women *Antony and Cleopatra*, when he persuaded her to spend first one, then dozens of nights in the room under the eaves with the east-facing porthole. When she understood that sexual ecstasy was more than an overinflated term. When, for the first time since she was seven years old, she screamed in pleasure. She had tumbled backwards into a remote unpeopled space, and later, lying side by side in bed, sheets to their waists like post-coital movie stars, they laughed at the din she had made. No one in the flat below, fortunately. He, cool long-haired Jack, told her it was the greatest compliment he'd ever received. She told him she could not imagine regaining the strength, in her spine, in her bones, to go back there again. Not if she was to return alive. But she did, often. She was young.

It was during this time, when they weren't in

bed together, that he thought he might further seduce her with jazz. He admired her playing but wanted to prise her loose from the tyranny of strict notation and long-dead genius. He played her Thelonious Monk's 'Round Midnight' and bought her the sheet music. It wasn't difficult to play. But her version, smooth and unaccented, sounded like an unremarkable piece by Debussy. That was fine, Jack told her. The great jazz masters adored and learned from him. She listened again, she persisted, she played what was in front of her, but she could not play jazz. No pulse, no instinct for syncopation, no freedom, her fingers numbly obedient to the time signature and notes as written. That was why she was studying law, she told her lover. Respect for the rules.

She gave up, but she did learn to listen, and it was Jarrett she came to admire above all others. She took Jack to hear him at the Colosseum in Rome. The technical facility, the effortless outpouring of lyrical invention as copious as Mozart's, and here it was again after so many years, still holding her to the spot, reminding her of who she and Jack once playfully were. The music was artfully chosen.

She went along the hall and paused again at the entrance to the sitting room. He had been busy. A couple of lamps with long-expired bulbs at last lit. Several candles around the room. The curtains drawn against the winter evening's light rain and, for the first time in more than a year, a well-established fire in the grate, logs as well as coal. Jack was standing by it with a bottle of champagne in his hand. In front of him, on a low table, a plate of prosciutto, olives and cheese.

He was wearing a black suit, white shirt without a tie. Still sleek. He came over, put in her hand a champagne flute and filled it, then poured his own. His expression was severe as they raised and touched glasses.

'We don't have much time.'

She took him to mean that soon they should be leaving to walk over to the Great Hall. It was madness to be drinking before a concert, but she didn't care. She took a second mouthful and followed him to the fire. He offered her the plate, she took a lump of parmesan, and they stood on each side of the fireplace, leaning against the mantelpiece. Like giant ornaments, she thought.

He said, 'Who knows how much. Not many years. Either we start living again, really living, or we give up and accept it's misery from here to the end.'

An old theme of his. *Carpe diem*. She raised her glass and said solemnly, 'To living again.'

She saw the slight shift in his expression. Relief and, beyond it, something more intense.

He refilled her glass. 'Concerning which, the dress is fabulous. You look beautiful.'

'Thank you.'

They held each other's gaze until there was nothing to do but go towards each other and kiss. They kissed again. His hand was lightly on the small of her back and he did not move it down across her thigh as he used to do. He was taking this in stages and his delicacy touched her. If a grand musical and social obligation had not been laid upon them, she did not doubt where this release would have led them. But her sheet music was behind her on the couch and their duty was to stay fully dressed. So they drew together tightly and kissed once more, then separated, picked up their glasses, touched them in silence and drank.

He sealed up the champagne with a cunning springed device she had given him many Christmases ago. 'For later,' he said and they laughed.

They fetched their coats and went out. To steady herself on her heels, she walked to the hall on her husband's arm, under his umbrella, which he gallantly held above her head and not his own.

'You're the performer,' he said. 'You're the one with the silk dress.'

A roar of small talk and laughter announced a crowd of a hundred and fifty or so, standing about with glasses of wine. The chairs were set out but no one was sitting yet, the Fazioli and a music stand were in position on stage. Members of Gray's, benchers, most of her professional and social life gathered in one place. For more than thirty years she had worked with and against dozens of people she could see. Various eminences, many from outside, from Lincoln's or Inner or Middle Temple — the Lord Chief Justice himself, some from the Court of Appeal, two Supreme Court justices, the Attorney General, a score of well-known barristers. The executives of the law, who settled fates and deprived citizens of their liberty, had a developed sense of humour and a passion for shop talk. The sound was deafening.

Within minutes, she and Jack had lost sight of each other. Someone came up and wanted help from him with some Latin. She was drawn into a circle of gossip about an eccentric friend of the Master of the Rolls. She hardly needed to move from where she stood. Friends came up to embrace her and wish her luck, others shook her hand. It had been a masterstroke of Pension, the Gray's Inn benchers' committee, to allow the concerts to be preceded by a party. Wine, Fiona hoped, might soften the critical faculties of the Wigmore Hall faction.

When a waiter with a silver tray came by, she was feeling too well to refuse. As she took a glass, Mark Berner appeared in her line of sight, some fifty feet and a hundred people away, wagging a forbidding finger. He was right, of course. She raised her glass to him and took a sip. A friend, a stalwart of the Queen's Bench, steered her over to meet a 'brilliant' barrister who happened to be his nephew. Watched over by the proud uncle, she asked solicitous questions of a thin young man with a pitiful stutter. She was beginning to long for livelier company when an old girlfriend from Middle Temple barged in, hugged her and stole her away to a circle of mutinous young women barristers who told her, though in humorous terms, that they weren't getting the quality work. It was going to the men.

Ushers were passing through the crowd announcing that the concert was about to begin. People moved with reluctance towards the chairs. It was difficult at first to exchange good wine and gossip for solemn music. But the glasses were being collected and the din was subsiding. She was making her way to the steps by the right-hand corner of the stage when she felt the touch of a hand on her shoulder and turned. It was Sherwood Runcie of the Martha Longman case. For some reason, in black tie. The uniform gave men of a certain age with bulging stomachs a trapped and pathetic air. He put his hand on her arm, wanting to impart an item of interest to her that had been kept out of the newspapers. She leaned in to catch his words. Her mind was already on the concert, her heartbeat already tightening, and she found it hard to concentrate on what he was saying, though she thought she had grasped it. Just as she was asking the judge to repeat himself, she became aware of Mark ahead of her, turning back to make impatient signs. She straightened, thanked Runcie and followed her tenor towards the stage.

While they stood at the foot of the steps waiting for their audience to settle and for their signal to go on, he said, 'Are you all right?'

'I'm fine. Why?'

'You look pale.'

'Mm.'

Automatically, she touched her hair with the fingertips of one hand. In the other was her music. She gripped it tighter. Did she look deranged? She reckoned up what she had drunk. No more than three sips of the white wine Mark had warned her off. About two glasses in all. She would be fine. He handed her towards the steps and as they went up to stand by the piano and dipped their heads by way of a bow, they met the sort of applause reserved for a home team. This was, after all, their fifth Christmas concert in the Great Hall.

When she sat down, arranged the music before her and made an adjustment to the piano stool, she drew a deep breath and softly exhaled to purge herself of the last scraps of recent conversation, of the stuttering barrister, the cheerful work-deprived young women. And Runcie. No. No time to think. Mark nodded at her to show he was ready, and immediately her fingers were summoning from the colossal instrument the gently rocking chords and her mind seemed to follow behind. The tenor's entry was perfect and within a few bars they were locked into a unity of purpose they had rarely touched in rehearsal, no longer concentrating on simply getting things right, but able to dissolve into the music without effort. It crossed her mind that she had drunk just the right quantity of wine. The smooth deep power of the Fazioli lifted her. It was as if she and Mark were being borne easily downstream on a current of notes. His voice sounded warmer to her ears, bang on the note, free of the tuneless vibrato he sometimes deployed, free to search out all the delight in Berlioz's setting of the 'Villanelle', and then, later, in the 'Lament', all the sorrow of the steeply falling line, *Ah! Sans amour s'en aller sur la mer!* Her own playing looked after itself. As her fingers touched the keys, she heard herself as though she were sitting at the back of the audience, as if all that was required of her was to

187

be present. Together, she and Mark entered the horizonless hyperspace of music-making, beyond time and purpose. She was only faintly aware that something waited for her return, for it lay far below her, an alien speck on a familiar landscape. Perhaps it wasn't there, perhaps it wasn't true.

They emerged as from a dream and stood side by side to face their audience again. The applause was loud, but it always was. In the spirit of Great Hall seasonal generosity, it was often louder for the ropier performances. It was only when she met Mark's glance and saw the shine in his eyes that she was certain that they had broken through the usual confines of amateur playing. They had actually brought something to the piece. If there was a woman in the audience he'd been wanting to impress, then she had been wooed in old-fashioned style and she surely must fall for him.

The silence fell abruptly as they took their places for the Mahler. Now she was on her own. The long introduction gave an impression of being invented by the pianist as it unfolded. With infinite patience, two notes tentatively sounded, then repeated and another added, then those three repeated, and only with the fourth did the line at last stretch luxuriantly upwards into one of the loveliest melodies the composer ever devised. She didn't feel unhappily exposed. She even managed to achieve what was second nature to first-rate pianists and coax from certain notes above middle C a bell-like sound. Elsewhere, she thought by her touch she could persuade her

188

listeners that they could hear the harp that belonged in the orchestral version. Right from his entry, Mark caught the spirit of tranquil resignation. For some reason he'd insisted on singing in English, not German, a freedom only granted to amateurs. The gain was the immediacy with which everyone understood a man retreating from the tumult. *I really am as good as dead to the world.* The couple sensed they were holding their audience, and their performance rose further. Fiona also knew she was moving at a stately pace towards something terrible. It was true, it wasn't true. She would only know when the music ceased and she confronted it.

Again, the applause, the faint bows, and now, the calls for an encore. There was even some foot-stamping, which began to grow louder. The performers looked at each other. There were tears in Mark's eyes. She felt her smile to be rigid. There was a metallic taste in her mouth as she turned back to the piano stool and the audience quietened. For seconds she kept her hands on her lap and her head down, refusing to glance across at her partner. From their selection of pieces committed to memory, they had already agreed on Schubert's 'An die Musik'. An old favourite. It never failed. She placed her hands in preparation on the keys but still she did not look up. The silence in the hall was complete, and finally she began. The ghost of Schubert may have blessed the introduction she played, but the rising three notes, a broken chord tenderly echoed lower, and again lower still, then resolving, belonged to another hand. In the quiet reiterated notes that pulsed in the background there may have been a gesture towards Berlioz. Who knew? Even Mahler's song, in its melancholy acceptance, may have subliminally helped Britten in this setting. Fiona sent no apology in Mark's direction. Her face was as rigid as her smile had been and she looked only at her hands. He had just seconds to rearrange his thoughts, but as he drew breath he was smiling and his tone was sweet, and sweeter still in the second verse.

In a field by the river my love and I did stand,
And on my leaning shoulder she laid her snow-white hand.
She bid me take life easy, as the grass grows on the weirs;
But I was young and foolish, and now am full of tears.

This was always a generous audience but it rarely rose to a standing ovation. That sort of thing was for pop concerts, as was shouting and whistling. But it rose as one now, with only a little hesitation from certain senior figures of the judiciary. Some younger enthusiasts shouted and whistled. But Mark Berner received the accolade alone, one hand resting on the piano, nodding and smiling in acknowledgement, and also watching with concern as his pianist walked quickly across the stage, gaze fixed on her feet, and went down the steps, pushing past the waiting members of the string quartet, and hurried towards the exit. It was generally assumed that the whole experience must have been unusually intense for her, and the benchers and their friends were sympathetic and clapped all the harder as she passed in front of them.

★　★　★

She found her coat and, careless of the fresh downpour, walked to the flat as quickly as she dared in high heels. In the sitting room, a couple of candles were as they had carelessly left them. Still in her coat, hair flattened to her scalp, water dribbling down her neck to the small of her back, she stood still, trying to remember a woman's name. So much had happened since she last thought of her. She recalled a face, she heard a voice, then it came back. Marina Greene. Fiona took her phone from her handbag and called. She apologised for calling out of hours. They spoke briefly, for there were screaming infants in the background and the young woman sounded tired and harassed. Yes, she could confirm it. Four weeks ago. She gave the few details she knew and said she was surprised that the judge had not been informed.

She remained standing in the same place, her gaze settled, for no particular reason, on the plate of food her husband had prepared, her mind a merciful blank. The music she had just played didn't resonate in her mind, the way it usually did. She had forgotten the concert. If it was neurologically possible not to think, she had no thoughts. Minutes passed. Impossible to know how many. At a sound, she turned. The fire was in its last throes and collapsing into the grate. She went over to it, knelt down and set about building it up, lifting fragments of wood and coal, with her fingers rather than the tongs, and placing them on and near the remains of the glowing heat. After three strokes of the bellows, a splinter of pine caught fire, which spread to two larger pieces as she watched. She moved closer and let the spectacle of tiny flames, their sideways bobbing and swiping movements across the surrounding blackness of coal, fill her vision.

At last, thoughts came in the form of two insistent questions. Why didn't you tell me? Why didn't you ask for my help? The answer came back in her own imagined voice. *I did*. She rose, aware of a pain in her hip as she went to her bedroom to retrieve the poem from the bedside table, where it had lain for six weeks. Its melodramatic tone, the puritanical suggestion that a bid for freedom, throwing the heavy cross in the river, receiving one chaste kiss, should be satanically inspired had deterred her from reading it again. There was something dank or suffocating about the Christian paraphernalia — the cross, the Judas tree, the trumpets. And she was the painted lady, the fish with rainbows on its scales, the treacherous creature that led the poet astray and kissed him. Yes, that kiss. It was her guilt that had kept her away.

She crouched down by the fire again and set the poem before her on the Bokhara rug. Her coal-dust fingerprints smudged the top of the

192

page. She went directly to the final verse — Jesus standing miraculously on the waters of the river, announcing that the fish was Satan in disguise and the poet 'must pay the fee'.

> Her kiss was the kiss of Judas, her kiss
>   betrayed my name.
> May he

She reached for her glasses on the table behind her and leaned closer in to follow the crossed-out and encircled words. 'Knife' was deleted, so was 'pay', 'Let him' and 'blame'. The word 'himself' was deleted, reinstated, deleted again. 'Mustn't' was replaced by 'must', and 'sinks' by 'drowns'. 'May' was by itself, without a balloon, floating above the fray, with an arrow indicating it should replace 'And'. She was getting the hang of his methods and his handwriting. And then she had it, she saw it plainly. There was even a meandering connecting line running between the chosen words. The Son of God had delivered a curse.

> May he who drowns my cross by his own
>   hand be slain.

When she heard the front door open, she didn't turn away, and this was how Jack glimpsed her as he passed by the sitting room on his way to the kitchen. He assumed she was tending the fire.

'Build it right up,' he called. And then, from further away, 'You were brilliant! Everyone loved it. And so moving!'

When he came back with the champagne and

two fresh glasses, she had stood to take off her coat and fling it over the back of a chair and remove her shoes. She was standing still in the centre of the room, waiting. He didn't notice her pallor as he gave her one of the glasses and she held it out to be filled.

'Your hair. Shall I get you a towel?'

'It'll dry.'

He removed the metal stopper and filled her glass, then his own, which he set down while he went over to the fire and emptied the coal scuttle over it and put on three large logs, wigwam style. He turned on the hi-fi and started the Jarrett again.

She murmured, 'Jack, not now.'

'Of course. After tonight! Stupid of me.'

She saw that his wish was to get back quickly to where they were before the concert, and she felt sorry for him. He was doing his best. Soon he would want to kiss her. He came back to her and in the silence, which had hissed in her ears the instant the hi-fi was off, they touched glasses and drank. Then he talked about her and Mark's performance, of his, Jack's, tears of pride when they all stood at the end, and what people were saying afterwards.

'It went well,' she said. 'I'm so glad it went well.'

He was not a musician, his taste was strictly for jazz and blues, but he spoke plausibly enough about the concert and remembered the pieces separately. *Les nuits d'été* was a revelation. He was especially moved by the 'Lament', he even understood the French. The Mahler he would

194

need to hear again for he sensed an enormous reservoir of feeling in it but he couldn't quite connect first time around. He was glad that Mark sang it in English. Everyone knew the urge to run from the world, few dared do it. She listened gravely, or appeared to, and gave short responses and nods. She felt like a hospital patient who longs for her kindly visitor to leave so she can resume being ill. The fire took, and Jack, noticing that she was shivering, guided her towards it and there he poured the rest of the champagne.

They had lived in the square a long time and he knew the Gray's Inn benchers almost as well as she did. He began to tell her about the people he had run into that evening. The square was tightly knit, the people in it fascinated them. The late-evening post-mortem was a feature of their lives together. It was easy for her to continue mumbling an occasional response. Jack remained in an elevated state, excited by her performance, and by what he thought lay ahead. He told her about a criminal lawyer who was setting up a free school with others. They needed a Latin translation for their motto, 'Every child a genius'. Three words maximum, short enough to be sewn onto a school blazer, under a heraldic phoenix rising from the ashes. It was a fascinating problem. Genius was an eighteenth-century concept, and Latin renderings of 'child' were mostly gender specific. Jack had come up with 'Cuiusque parvuli ingenium' — not quite as strong as genius but natural wit or ability would do nicely. At a pinch 'parvuli' could encompass

195

girls. Then the lawyer had asked him if he'd be interested in creating a lively Latin course for eleven- to sixteen-year-olds of mixed abilities. Challenging. Irresistible.

She listened without expression. No child of hers would ever wear such a wonderful badge. She was excessively vulnerable, she realised.

She said, 'That would be a good thing to do.'

He caught the flatness of her tone and looked at her differently.

'Something's up.'

'I'm all right.'

Then frowning as he recalled the question he had failed to ask, he said, 'Why did you walk off at the end?'

She hesitated. 'It was too much for me.'

'When they all stood? I almost cracked up completely.'

'It was the last song.'

'The Mahler.'

' 'The Salley Gardens'.'

He assumed an amused, disbelieving look. He had heard her perform it with Mark a dozen times before. 'How so?'

There was also in his manner a touch of impatience. He was wanting to fulfil the promise of a wonderful evening, to put their marriage back together, kiss her, open another bottle, take her to bed, make everything easy between them once more. She knew him well, she saw all this and, again, she felt sorry for him, but she felt it from a great distance.

She said, 'A memory. From the summer.'

'Yes?' His tone was only mildly curious.

'A young man played that tune to me on his violin. He was just learning. It was in a hospital. I sang along. I think we made a bit of a din. Then he wanted to play it again, but I had to leave.'

Jack was in no mood for puzzles. He struggled to keep the irritation out of his voice. 'Start again. Who was this?'

'A very strange and beautiful young man.' She spoke vaguely, trailing away.

'And?'

'I suspended proceedings while I went to his bedside to see him. You remember. A Jehovah's Witness, very ill, refusing treatment. It was in the papers.'

If he needed reminding it was because he was installed in Melanie's bedroom at the time. Otherwise, they would have discussed the case.

He said staunchly, 'I think I remember it.'

'I gave the hospital leave to treat him and he recovered. The judgment had . . . it had an effect on him.'

They stood as they had earlier, on each side of the fire, which now gave off a fierce heat. She stared down into the flames. 'I think . . . I think he had strong feelings for me.'

Jack set down his empty glass. 'Go on.'

'When I was on circuit he followed me up to Newcastle. And I . . . ' She wasn't going to tell him what happened there, and then she changed her mind. No point concealing anything now. 'He walked through the rain to find me and . . . I did something so stupid. In the hotel. I don't know what I was . . . I kissed him. I *kissed* him.'

He took a step away from the fire's heat, or

from her. She no longer cared.

She whispered. 'He was the sweetest fellow. He wanted to come and live with us.'

'Us?'

Jack Maye had come of age in the 1970s among all its currents of thought. He had taught in a university his entire adult life. He knew all about the illogic of double standards, but knowing could not protect him. She saw the anger in his face, tightening the muscles along his jaw, hardening his eyes.

'He thought I could change his life. I suppose he wanted to make me into a kind of guru. He thought I could . . . He was so earnest, so hungry for life, for everything. And I didn't . . . '

'So you kissed him and he wanted to live with you. What are you trying to tell me?'

'I sent him away.' She shook her head and for the moment she couldn't speak.

Then she looked at Jack. He stood well away from her, feet apart, arms crossed, his still-handsome, good-natured face stiff with anger. A wisp of silvery chest hair curled up through his open-necked shirt. She had sometimes seen him tease it up with a comb. That the world should be filled with such detail, such tiny points of human frailty, threatened to crush her and she had to look away.

Only now, when it stopped, were they aware of the rain that had been beating at the windows.

Into this deeper silence he said, 'So what's happened? Where is he now?'

She spoke in a quiet monotone. 'I heard it tonight from Runcie. Some weeks ago his

198

leukaemia came back and he was taken into hospital. He refused the transfusion they wanted to give him. That was his decision. He was eighteen and there was nothing anyone could do. He refused and his lungs filled with blood and he died.'

'So he died for his faith.' Her husband's voice was cold.

She looked at him without comprehension. She realised that she had not explained herself at all, that there was so much she hadn't told him.

'I think it was suicide.'

For some seconds neither spoke. They heard voices, laughter and footsteps in the square. The musical event was breaking up.

He cleared his throat softly. 'Were you in love with him, Fiona?'

The question undid her. She let out a terrible sound, a smothered howl. 'Oh Jack, he was just a child! A boy. A lovely boy!' And she began to weep at last, standing by the fire, her arms hanging hopelessly at her sides, while he watched, shocked to see his wife, always so self-contained, at the furthest extremes of grief.

She was beyond speech and the crying would not stop and she could not bear any longer to be seen. She stooped to gather up her shoes and hurried across the room in her stockinged feet and along the hallway. The further away from him she was, the louder she cried. She reached her bedroom, slammed the door behind her and, without turning on the light, fell onto the bed and sank her face into a pillow.

Half an hour later, when she woke, climbing in a dream an interminable vertical ladder from the depths, she had no memory of falling asleep. Still in a daze, she lay on her side, facing the door. Along its bottom edge, a slit of light from the hallway was reassuring. But the imagined scenes before her were not. Adam falling ill again, returning home weakened to his loving parents, meeting the kindly elders, returning to the faith. Or using it as the perfect cover to destroy himself. *May he who drowns my cross by his own hand be slain.* In low light she saw him as she had on her visit to intensive care. The pale thin face, the shaded purple under huge violet eyes. The caked tongue, arms like sticks, so ill, so determined on death, so full of charm and life, pages of his poetry spilling over the bed, pleading with her to stay and play their song again when she had to return to court.

There, in court, with the authority and dignity of her position, she offered him, instead of death, all of life and love that lay ahead of him. And protection against his religion. Without faith, how open and beautiful and terrifying the world must have seemed to him. With that thought she slipped back into a deeper sleep and woke minutes later to the singing and the sighing of the gutters. Would it ever stop raining? She saw the solitary figure making his way up the drive of Leadman Hall, bent against the rainstorm, finding a way in the dark, hearing the falling branches. He must have seen ahead the lights in

200

the house and known she was there. He shivered in an outhouse, wondering, waiting for his chance to talk to her, risking everything in the pursuit of — what exactly? And believing he could get it from a woman in her sixtieth year who had risked nothing in life beyond a few reckless episodes in Newcastle a long time ago. She should have been flattered. And ready. Instead, on a powerful and unforgivable impulse, she kissed him, then sent him away. Then ran away herself. Failed to answer his letters. Failed to decipher the warning in his poem. How ashamed she was now of her petty fears for her reputation. Her transgression lay beyond the reach of any disciplinary panel. Adam came looking for her and she offered nothing in religion's place, no protection, even though the Act was clear, her paramount consideration was his welfare. How many pages in how many judgments had she devoted to that term? Welfare, well-being, was social. No child is an island. She thought her responsibilities ended at the court-room walls. But how could they? He came to find her, wanting what everyone wanted, and what only free-thinking people, not the supernatural, could give. Meaning.

When she shifted position she felt against her face the pillow wet and cold. Fully awake now, she pushed it aside to reach for another, and was surprised to touch a warm body stretched out alongside her, at her back. She turned. Jack lay with his head propped on his hand. With the other he pushed her hair clear of her eyes. It was a tender gesture. By the light from the hall she could just see his face.

He said simply, 'I've been watching you sleep.'

After a while, a long while, she whispered, 'Thank you.'

Then she asked him if he would still love her once she had told him the whole story. It was an impossible question, for he knew almost nothing yet. She suspected he would try to persuade her that her guilt was misplaced.

He put his hand on her shoulder and drew her to him. 'Of course I will.'

They lay face to face in the semi-darkness, and while the great rain-cleansed city beyond the room settled to its softer nocturnal rhythms and their marriage uneasily resumed, she told him in a steady quiet voice of her shame, of the sweet boy's passion for life, and her part in his death.

Acknowledgements

This novel would not exist without Sir Alan Ward, lately of the Court of Appeal, a judge of great wisdom, wit and humanity. My story has its origins in a case he presided over in the High Court in 1990, and another in the Court of Appeal in 2000. However, my characters, their views, personalities and circumstances, bear no relation to any of the parties in either of those cases. I owe a huge debt of gratitude to Sir Alan for advising me on various legal technicalities as well the everyday existence of a High Court judge. I'm grateful to him also for taking time to read a draft and make comments. I lay claim to any inaccuracies.

Similarly, I have drawn on a superbly written judgment by Sir James Munby in 2012 and, again, my characters are entirely fictional and bear no resemblance to the participants in that case.

I am grateful for the advice of Bruce Barker-Benfield of the Bodleian Library, and of James Wood of Doughty Street Chambers. I am also grateful to have read 'Managing Without Blood', a thoughtful and wide-ranging thesis by the barrister and Jehovah's Witness Richard Daniel. Once again, I am indebted to Annalena McAfee, Tim Garton Ash and Alex Bowler for their close readings and helpful suggestions.

Ian McEwan

We do hope that you have enjoyed reading this large print book.

Did you know that all of our titles are available for purchase?

We publish a wide range of high quality large print books including:
Romances, Mysteries, Classics
General Fiction
Non Fiction and Westerns

Special interest titles available in large print are:
The Little Oxford Dictionary
Music Book
Song Book
Hymn Book
Service Book

Also available from us courtesy of Oxford University Press:
Young Readers' Dictionary
(large print edition)
Young Readers' Thesaurus
(large print edition)

For further information or a free brochure, please contact us at:
Ulverscroft Large Print Books Ltd.,
The Green, Bradgate Road, Anstey,
Leicester, LE7 7FU, England.
Tel: (00 44) 0116 236 4325
Fax: (00 44) 0116 234 0205

Other titles published by Ulverscroft:

WHAT WAS PROMISED

Tobias Hill

Post-war London: Children run wild on East End bombsites, while their elders strive for better lives in a country beggared by victory. Clarence and Bernadette Malcolm have come five thousand miles in search of prosperity, but find that the Mother Country is not at all what it was promised to be; Solly and Dora Lazarus, too, are strangers in a strange land, struggling to belong even as they try to make sense of their past; and Michael and Mary Lockhart take with both hands all that the world owes them, whatever the cost. In the street markets and tenements of Bethnal Green the three families live and work together in uneasy harmony, until Michael shatters the balance between them, his hunger for betterment changing the courses of all their lives over decades and generations.

REMEMBER ME LIKE THIS

Bret Anthony Johnston

Four years have passed since Justin Campbell's disappearance, a tragedy that rocked the small town of Southport, Texas. Did he run away? Did he drown in the bay? As the Campbells search for answers, they struggle to hold what's left of their family together. Then one afternoon, the impossible happens. The police call to report that Justin has been found in a nearby town, and he appears to be fine. And though the reunion is a miracle, Justin's homecoming exposes the deep rifts that have diminished his family; the wounds they all carry that may never fully heal. When a reversal of fortune lays bare the family's greatest fears — and offers perhaps their only hope for recovery — each of them must fight to keep the ties that bind them from permanently tearing apart.